I0590761

# RELOAD FASTER

# RELOAD FASTER

## I FEAR NO EVIL BOOK THREE

MARTHA CARR
MICHAEL ANDERLE

DISRUPTIVE IMAGINATION

RELOAD FASTER TEAM

## Thanks to the JIT Readers

Mary Morris
James Caplan
John Ashmore
Kelly Bowerman
Peter Manis
Joshua Ahles
Daniel Weigert
Kelly O'Donnell
Paul Westman
Larry Omans
Micky Cocker

*If we've missed anyone, please let us know!*

*From Martha*

To everyone who still believes in magic
and all the possibilities that holds.
To all the readers who make this
entire ride so much fun.
And to my son, Louie and so many wonderful friends who
remind me all the time of what
really matters and how wonderful
life can be in any given moment.

*From Michael*

To Family, Friends and
Those Who Love
To Read.
May We All Enjoy Grace
To Live The Life We Are
Called.

S hay pressed her back against the smooth cement wall of the darkened La Brea Tar Pits museum, Peyton's voice screaming in her ear.

"Tone it down or I'm ditching this thing," she whispered.

"Sorry, that one was a little close for me."

"Your ass isn't even on the line."

Peyton was sitting back in the safety of the warehouse, watching everything on a computer monitor. He was wearing a safari outfit with red, white and blue suspenders. It was his homage to dinosaurs and to big oil.

"That pin camera makes it feel like I'm there. I heard that bullet whizz right past your ear!" He stood up, excited, knocking the chair back.

"Send up the drone and tell me where they are now."

Shay could see from her position below, the blinking red light in the darkness as the drone disappeared just over the edge of the tall building.

"Okay," said Peyton, "there's one crawling up the fire

escape toward the roof and two moving down the sidewalk. Tell me again how you managed to piss them off?"

Shay grimaced and made a mental note to shortsheet Peyton's bed with a nice mixture of spiders. "I didn't piss anyone off. I got to the treasure ahead of them. Hometown girl, I know the turf better." They were definitely out of town hired help. Goons with guns.

Peyton had found her a job digging out an old amulet near the La Brea Tar Pits in Los Angeles. She would be home before dinner if it weren't for the hired army who had the same idea at the same time.

Shay would have to look into that later. See if someone betrayed her or it was just dumb luck.

"Well, they came prepared because they're crawling all over," said Peyton, a buzzing voice in Shay's ear. "Gonna call them the Ant Hill gang."

"I'm sure that won't inspire them to put a bullet through you."

"From the looks of things, Shay they don't need inspiration. Oh shit, get out of there. The guy on the roof is coming over to your side. Time to move."

Shay checked the bag slung across her chest and scanned the area for the best way to get out of there with the least amount of visibility. At least she was able to draw them away to a more deserted location.

The coordinates for the amulet put it closer to Wilshire Boulevard, still hopping even at three in the morning. Just a different kind of crowd.

Peyton's voice, still excited, flew back into her brain. "My idea of a disguise turned out to be brilliant."

"That wasn't a novel idea. I was already going through the warehouse."

"Well, I gave it the theme. School marm was a good choice. You managed to get the hell out of there without pulling out your gun."

"Who says marm," Shay hissed under her breath as she ditched the costume. "And it's not a marm, it's average suburban white woman."

Underneath Shay was wearing an all-black, tight fitting suit; her first choice when tomb raiding. She slid the black hood up over her head, tucking in her hair and made a run for it from the back of the building.

She looked back in time to see someone dart behind some trees. The tomb raider raised her gun, still making her way across the open area. Not a good place to stop and reconnaissance anything.

"Average suburban white woman on Wilshire during the day would make you stand out like a sore thumb," said Peyton. "Where's the Gucci? But at night, it has *I need a drug buy* written all over it. Brilliant! Where are you running to? All I see are trees."

Shay heard the buzz of the distant drone and angrily spat out, "Fly that damn mechanical gnat in the other direction, away from me!"

"Right, good call. Or roger that. Fuck!"

Shay heard the shouts in the distance behind her. "What? Now you stop talking?"

"Sorry, swallowed my gum. Uh, Shay, they've brought in reinforcements."

"Why do they want this amulet so badly? The price

doesn't warrant this much attention. You did research the amulet's history, right?"

"Pshew, yes, of course I did."

Shay could hear the sound of frantic typing. *Snakes in his bed, definitely snakes.*

Shay glanced over her shoulder and saw something run across the open space, diagonally away from her. She thought about taking a shot but too many people came out at night to play in this city. She wasn't going to take the chance of killing a nosey bystander.

Old life protocol versus new life.

"Great, now I have to keep track of two directions." Shay's rented Jeep was parked a mile back behind the Park La Brea apartments under a burned-out streetlight. Once she was past the open ground it would get easier to move along the smaller streets and get to her car unnoticed.

First, she had to get a few more hundred yards.

"What's that? What's going on? Okay, I found it. Not my fault," said Peyton.

"No one likes excuses. This is right about where I would have just shot you in the old days, just so I wouldn't hear it."

"Well, thank goodness times change. Okay, this was hard to find. Obscure little mention on the dark web. Right... excuse... The amulet was part of a set of jewelry once owned by some ancient Oriceran. I mean ancient, even for La Brea Tar Pits. Dropped there a few gate openings ago. Really dark and ancient magic was poured into it just before this Oriceran queen bought it."

Shay took off at a run just as klieg lights went on

behind her, scoping the ground. They were ditching subtle altogether.

She ducked lower to the ground and kept moving. The figure to the left took off running as well, easily passing her in the distance. "What the hell?" she whispered.

"This way," a deep voice shouted as the growing crowd of mercenaries focused their attention on the back grounds of the museum.

Getting closer...

"What exactly does the damn thing do?" Shay hissed, running as fast as she could.

"This says it has the power to bestow magic on its owner. Something weird here about if it wants to. I don't know. A lot of this was translated from an old Oriceran language."

"No wonder they want it so badly."

The sound of dirt bikes coming over the hill filled the air.

"Shit, I'm gonna need a few clever moves to get out of this one." Shay stood up and ran full out, grateful for all the hours of training. She was going to need it.

She kept her focus on the buildings ahead and a chance at ducking in somewhere, not looking back even as she could hear the bikes getting closer.

She felt a hand wrap around her ankle, startling her even as she put out her hands to break her hard fall. The wind knocked out of her but she was trained for something like this too. She rolled over, ready to kick her assailant in the face, the hand still gripping her ankle.

"Shay, what was that loud thump? Shay? The camera's gone dark." Peyton's voice was pleading for an answer.

Shay hesitated when she saw the girl's face in the dim light. The girl was partially out of a grass-covered hole, doing her best to pull Shay inside. Shay didn't need to ask questions, not right now. She easily slid herself inside the opening as the girl let go, pulling the cover over both of them.

Shay found herself standing on the rungs of a metal ladder, squeezed next to the girl as they scrambled down. They both paused when the bikes squealed overhead, followed by the sound of running footsteps.

"Where the fuck did she go?" An angry male voice shouted. Shay couldn't help smiling.

"Police helicopter coming."

"We pay them more than enough. Maybe they can spot her."

"Who the hell is she?" Another voice shouted, just as angry.

The girl looked at Shay and pulled out a small flashlight, lighting the way. "Come on, we better get out of here while we still can. Not too many people know there's an old abandoned nuclear escape tunnel back here, but better safe than sorry."

Peyton's voice had gone silent. Shay looked around at the cement walls, guessing they were pretty thick if they were built to withstand a nuclear blast. No signal would penetrate that.

"Who are you?" Shay adjusted the bag and moved behind the girl as they entered a large, circular cement opening that stretched ten feet over Shay's head.

"I could ask the same thing. I go by Lily. It's a name I gave myself. Backgrounds don't matter down here."

"Down here?"

They hurried down the wide tunnel, splashing through brackish water, making two left turns and then a right. "You know your way around down here pretty well."

"I should, I've been living down here for over a year."

They came into an even larger tunnel just as a small gathering of teenagers scattered into other openings, disappearing down other tunnels.

"I had a feeling that would happen. You're a little old and dressed like a remake from Mission Impossible. They were gonna run first, slap me around for answers later."

"My kind of crowd, and what the hell do you mean by old? I'm in my twenties."

"Exactly... old. This is one of the best underground hangouts for people like me. Under twenties with nowhere else to go. Protected from the elements, out of harms way. Pretty good circumstances."

Shay pulled out her own flashlight and shone the beam around the tunnel. "Sure, if damp smells and hard ground are your thing."

"Better than where I came from. Father got picked up by a bounty hunter. Dark magic was his thing. Mom disappeared a long time ago."

"You're magical?" Shay shone her flashlight on Lily. Long gray hair hung down to her waist. "You're a gray elf. I've heard of your kind. I thought you were all about good."

"You mean my father? Yeah, well, there has to be one to prove the rule, right? Mom was human. That put me on the outs with the rest of my kind. They don't take well to mixing blood." Lily found a tattered sleeping bag spread out over cardboard and a tarp and sat down on the ground.

Shay tilted her head and took in the teenager. "That your corner of this Eden?"

"Don't knock it till you've tried it. Yeah, this is all mine. Everyone knows not to touch any of it. I'd know who did it. Part of my weird powers."

Shay went and crouched down next to the pile of books. Hemingway, Kafka, Harry Potter. "Interesting mix."

"Yeah, well, thieves can't always be choosers. I like to read and I need a steady supply of books."

Shay stood back up, brushing the dirt off her hands. "What weird powers do you have, exactly?"

Lily looked up at her, narrowing her eyes. "I know that look. Like I've suddenly become a useful tool. No thanks, not interested. Look, I saved your life up there because I don't like watching the steel boots take out a woman, especially a kick ass one. I saw what you did to a bunch of them up there."

"And you still managed to get ahead of me. Pretty impressive."

"I know the territory better than you. Micro-knowledge of the area and they weren't looking for me."

"And…"

"And my weird powers. I sometimes get glimpses of the future. Only about fifteen minutes in advance and not always. Must be part of that mixing blood thing. A little unreliable." Lily patted her belly, her gray hair falling over her shoulder, covering half her face. Her deep gray eyes shone in the light.

"I get a gut feeling that tells me it's legit. I saw what you were up against and I was in the mood to help. Those mindless thugs can go fuck themselves."

"You don't care what I was doing up there?"

"Not even a little."

Shay weighed the options in her head, wondering what to do when she saw something. She leaned down and reached out to turn over the piece of metal, but Lily was faster and snatched it out of her reach.

"That's mine," Lily said, breathing a little hard.

"How did you get that?" Shay could feel her heart rate pick up and she took in longer breaths to control it. Last time she saw that artifact it was hanging off the belt of the Ice Witch. How did a kid get it off the witch that came close to taking down Shay?

"Weird powers. I needed it. I took it."

"It's not that simple."

"Close to it. Bitch didn't anticipate my move. Got this nice little scar for my troubles." Lily held up her arm. There was a long, thin red scar that ran from her wrist to her elbow.

"Ice did that." Shay's mind was working on a solution.

Lily's eyes grew wider and she sat up. "You've seen her. Do you know where I can find her?"

"No, and for your sake you should stop looking for her. Why were you so desperate you'd tangle with her for that artifact? What does it do?"

"It's not what it does, so much. It's who it belonged to. It was my father's. That's the bitch who turned him in. I plan to even the score."

"That's something I can understand. Interested in a trade?"

The terms didn't take long. Shay agreed to help Lily with her quest in exchange for Lily's help on a few missions. No social services, no cops and Lily could change her mind after a month. Shay would put her up in one of the warehouses and feed her. Hell, she was already feeding Peyton. *What was one more mouth?*

Shay helped her gather up what there was of her things, careful not to touch the metal artifact.

"What does that thing do, anyway?"

"It's a kind of divining rod. It can help find things."

Shay smiled as they came to a ladder. "You and I are going to get along just fine, one way or another."

Lily scrambled up the stairs first, getting to the top in lightning speed.

*Weird powers, I guess*, thought Shay. *She's got fast twitch reflexes.* Shay adjusted the old backpack, heavy with books and easily made the climb to the top as Lily pushed open a hatch.

They came out on a side street only blocks from Shay's rental car.

"Where the fuck are you?!" Peyton was full on shouting in her ear. "Oh my God, I've lost her. Brownstone will literally skin me and make me a rug! My life is over. How do you hide from a Level Six bounty hunter? Oh Shay!" He let out a gulp and pounded his chest.

"Little dramatic don't you think?"

Lily looked up as Shay crossed her arms and took a look around. Nothing was stirring except for the rats.

"Shay? Shay! You're alive! Are you captured? Should I call someone?" Peyton wiped his sweaty palms on his pants and silently thanked the heavens he would get to keep his skin another day.

"I'm good, we're good. Peyton, if you're going to do ops in my ear you're going to need to develop a calmer persona. Screaming goat isn't going to cut it."

"Who are you talking to? Never mind, gadgets, I get it. We have to keep moving. This area is never safe and those guys didn't give up that easily."

"Shay, who are you talking to? What's going on there?" Lily scanned the area.

"Peyton, focus. Is the drone still in the air? Can you tell me where the herd ran off to?"

"Sure, sure. Answers later. Still on a mission. Damn, that was a close one. I mean, I thought… okay, okay. Looks like they've broken into smaller units and have spread out over the area. They're wallet slapping the homeless and spreading around some money."

"Time to go," said Shay. She took off at a run, taking the route she had planned out for the mission. It took her on a slightly longer route back to the car but was under the darkest parts of any street and away from cameras.

Lily easily kept up, not even breathing hard and it took them no time to get to the Jeep. They loaded Lily's things in the back and slid in the car.

Lily suddenly looked up, her eyebrows shooting up as her eyes moved rapidly back and forth.

"Hit the gas. We've only got a few minutes before this place will be crawling with men and guns."

"Men and guns. Put one in their hands and they feel obligated to shoot out something. A vision I take it?"

"They look more like rapidly changing snapshots. Told you, not perfect."

Shay heard the sounds of cars approaching as she maneuvered the Jeep out of the parking lot and took off in the opposite direction. "Not exactly fifteen minutes of lead time."

Lily shrugged her shoulders and put her feet up on the dashboard.

Clearly Lily and her weird powers were a work in progress. Still, she pulled one over on the Ice Witch. Pretty badass... and useful.

Shay ditched the car and they took off, easily running the mile to where her sportscar was parked in a garage. Purity Solutions, the clean up service would pick the car up for her, wipe it down of all prints and any sign she was ever in it and return to the rental place. A business expense.

Lily was silent for the entire ride, watching the scenery

go by as Shay sped as fast as she dared, slowing down as they got closer to Warehouse Two.

The roll top door slid up as Shay pulled inside, shutting off the engine. "Come on, there's a bed you can use tonight."

"In here? This is a warehouse."

"And above ground, and clean, and has an endless supply of pizza."

Peyton came running over, his hair standing up in tufts on the top of his head from where he had been panicking and running his hands through it.

Shay got out, took one look at him and started to laugh. Just giggles at first but soon she was bent over, catching her breath and every time she looked up, she started laughing again.

Peyton frowned, crossing his arms over his chest even as he glanced over at Lily who waited patiently by the car, not saying a word.

"Okay, an emotional release from not dying, I get it."

Shay straightened up, a smirk still on her face. "Not almost dying. Used to that, hell, that's kind of old hat. You look like a cross between a punk rocker and a failed safari guide. It's not a good look."

Lily put her hand over her mouth, hiding the start of a smile. Not fast enough for Peyton to miss it.

"Who's this? We taking in boarders?"

"*You* aren't doing anything because *you* don't own this place. Lily meet Peyton, he's my tech guy. Peyton, meet Lily. She's going to train with me to go on a few missions." Shay purposely left out any mention of magic. A conversation for a different day.

Peyton's mouth dropped open and stayed that way for a moment as he looked her up and down. Lily returned the gesture and gave him the finger as she passed by him, following Shay.

"What is it with the women around here? All so hostile."

Shay rested the leather bag she'd been protecting next to Peyton's computer. "Tell the buyer, we got the artifact and it's safe and sound, but I want a bonus for almost getting killed. And Peyton, next time you don't miss the details, including why there was an army out there at the same time. I want answers on that."

Shay went into the office and looked around, clearing books off the couch. "Lily, you can stay here till we figure out something better. There's a full shower and toiletries in the bathroom. Peyton can show you where it is. You can use anything you find in there."

"Not my Sauvage." Peyton pointed in the general direction of the large bathroom. Like anything else Shay did, the bathroom was done to her exacting standards with a heated marble floor and an expansive walk-in shower.

"Is that what that smell is?" asked Lily, wrinkling her nose.

"No, that's Italian sausage pizza. Very funny. I suppose you're hungry too."

"How did you two meet?" asked Lily, one eyebrow arched.

"She scooped me up off the street just ahead of a few assassins."

"A few?" yelled Shay as Peyton did his best to ignore her.

"What about you?"

"I saved her ass… just in front of an army of them."

Peyton looked back at Shay who shrugged. He looked at Lily and held up his hand for a high-five. "Respect, sister. I'm usually getting her into tight places."

Shay listened to them get back to bickering all the way to the bathroom. "Like I opened a nursery for the gifted," she muttered. "But the Ice Witch. Peyton is right, some respect."

Lily devoured half of a pizza and laid down on the couch, fast asleep in minutes. Peyton went back to quietly working at the computer, occasionally glancing over his shoulder at her.

Shay got up to leave, glad to be headed back to her townhouse as Peyton eased out of his chair and caught up to her.

"That was a bold trust move on your part. Didn't know you had it in you."

"I did the same thing with you, if you recall."

"Not even. You did your research on me, first. You picked this one off the pile and said, come on. What if she was lying about everything?"

"Then I'll shoot her."

"I'd laugh because you're kidding but…"

"Just have her ready to go tomorrow by seven a.m… Her training starts early if she's going to earn her keep. She's got a lot of raw talent…"

"And is magical. Yeah, I noticed. I can see what she is, a gray elf."

"Partial. She's going to need some training so that she doesn't fuck up on her first mission."

"Always thinking. I'll have her up and full of Eggos by the time you arrive."

Shay slid into her car, resting against the leather seat.

"Hey Shay, the buyer's already replied. He wants to meet up with you as soon as possible to get the artifact and lock it away in some dark hole where it'll never be seen again. He said he'd be at the diner at seven. Goes by the name of Samuel." Peyton walked over to the car, holding up the bag. He handed it over to Shay along with two slices of pizza wrapped in foil. "For a snack in the bathtub. See, I do know you."

"Then I'll be by here by eight," Shay said with a laugh.

---

"You could have given me a heads up." Shay looked across the Formica table at the light elf as he devoured the plate of bacon and eggs. "Do all elves eat like that?"

Shay made a mental note to double the order for the grocery store. Same clean up service picked it up for her and dropped it off, no questions asked and no trace to her.

"What? Maybe..." Samuel wiped the grease off his chin. "Magic burns a lot of calories."

"You hope." Shay took a sip of her black coffee. "I think I may envy that more than the magic. You sure you can lock away this artifact for good this time?"

"That's the goal. It was part of some vault that kept dangerous artifacts and was one of their first deposits.

Thing was destroyed about twenty years ago. I'll be taking it back as soon as I leave here."

"Make sure no one follows you home."

"I have my own style of transportation. Portals cut down on tails. Was there much trouble retrieving it?"

"You could say that. A small army of mercenaries showed up, armed for a war. Want to tell me how they got tipped off?"

"Same way we did, I imagine. Confidential informant playing both sides of the street. Don't worry, he's being dealt with. My partner is paying him a visit."

"Your partner cleans up after you?"

"Not so much. She's a bounty hunter, and it was her informant. He'll be sorry he crossed her. Won't happen again." He took an oversized bite of the biscuit.

"Did you want to order more?"

Samuel looked up and smiled, the biscuit bulging in his cheek. "No, I'm good. Money's in your account. You do good work. Wasn't sure you could pull off this one and you came away without a scratch."

"I had help... an assistant."

"That Brownstone guy?"

"No, he's more of a partner. A young gray elf. I'm training her."

"Smart. I've found it useful to go into battle next to an ally or two."

"Let's keep that between us for now."

Samuel stopped chewing and looked at her, narrowing his eyes. "Tell no one, got it."

"I appreciate it."

"No problem. You're sorting things out, I get it. Till we

meet again." Samuel wiped his hands on the napkin and picked up the bag, heading for the men's room.

"You sure you should take that with you to the bathroom? I'll watch it for you."

"I'm making my exit back there," he said, smiling. "Less of an audience. I already took care of the bill."

Shay watched him stride back to the men's room and heard the sound of sparks as the light elf quickly made his departure. She hit the app on her phone and checked her bank account, quickly moving the money into one of her other accounts. Business was picking up and business was good.

Shay rolled into the warehouse long enough to pick up Lily and roll her eyes at Peyton's outfit. He was dressed all in white in celebration of some rock star's annual white party. "I may not be able to go this year, since I'm supposed to be dead, but I can still celebrate," he had said.

As they pulled out, Lily started to put her feet on Shay's dashboard until she saw the withering look.

"This one's not a rental. Feet on the ground."

"What did he mean he's supposed to be dead?"

"Long story. He's not very popular with his family of origin."

"A lot of that going around." Lily looked down at her hands. Shay couldn't help thinking of Alison. They were about the same age.

"It's not my business, but why do you want to take out

the Ice Witch for ratting out your father? I got the impression he wasn't the nicest guy."

"It's complicated and he stuck by me all those years after my mother bailed."

"I think that's called parenting. It's what you do."

"Well, he did it half-assed a lot of the time, but he was trying. More than most got who live in that tunnel. The bitch had no right to take him from me."

"He must have gotten in her way."

"Something like that. Where are we headed? Gold's Gym?"

Shay knew Lily was changing the subject but let it go. "Not even. It's something I put together in another warehouse."

"Another warehouse? Tomb raiding must be paying off for you."

"I've been an entrepreneur of sorts for years."

"Of sorts... I know what that means. Never mind, I know when to not ask questions."

"That's a relief. Peyton doesn't possess that off switch."

"I noticed. I think it's his secret weapon. He flies so many questions at you, you answer them and before you know it, he's got what he came for."

"He is clever in a beady-eyed costumed sort of way."

Shay stopped for coffee on the way, introducing Lily to a proper roast and a good doughnut, reminding herself that this was not Alison. She didn't know anything about her. Still, Brownstone had taken the same chance at just the right moment for the Drow Princess and look what happened. Shay shook her head. *Slow down Carson.*

She rolled into the warehouse and waited for the door

to shut before showing Lily where she could change. "There should be something in there that will fit you. We'll take it easy today and let you get acclimated."

Lily walked toward the changing room, her head tilted back, staring at the obstacle course spread out around the large warehouse.

She came back out minutes later in a tight black tank top and black pants with an orange stripe down the side, and bare feet.

"None of the shoes back there fit you? We can fix that later."

"Don't need them. I do better in bare feet."

"Suit yourself. Let's find out what you can do. Where do you want to start?"

Shay was pleasantly surprised when Lily grabbed onto one of the long, thick ropes and easily shimmied up midway, reaching out for a ring and swinging hand over hand, ring to ring to the climbing wall. It had taken Shay at least a week to master the same move.

"Twitch muscles," Shay muttered, watching Lily scramble higher on the wall without a harness. She reached out for a bar, her hand slipping for a moment and she reflexively put out her other hand, saving herself from falling a long way to the surface below.

Shay felt herself take in a sharp intake of breath but didn't move, waiting to see what Lily would do next. She pulled herself over to the jumping spider walls, firmly suspended from the ceiling. Her hands and feet were spread out between the thick plexiglass, pulling herself toward the top.

Lily stopped halfway and even from the floor Shay could see how hard she was breathing.

This may be a short experiment, thought Shay. Should have known better. Strong willed teenager plus high-end gym. Not a good match.

Lily's arms were shaking, and she gritted her teeth. She let out a roar as she steadily moved her arms and legs upward till she got to the top and a ledge where she could sit and take a break.

Shay slowly let out the breath she was holding. "Not bad, but if you're going to go on missions with me, you're going to have to learn to wait for instructions," Shay shouted. Still, she was impressed. Girl has spit and vinegar. Shay let herself smile, just a little. It was not going to be easy to get to know this teenager. She had more layers than Alison, but there was something there to work with. Soon enough.

## 3

The red-rock desert extended below Shay as she sailed through the air. She shifted her body to adjust her paraglider to keep the landing zone on the mesa in front of her. A glance back showed the three dark forms of her enemies approaching quickly.

*Damn it. So much for losing them in Sedona.*

Shay hissed under her breath as the top of the mesa grew larger. She needed to be on the ground. A gunfight in the air wasn't a bright idea, even for her.

The tense seconds ticked by until her feet hit the rock. As she unbuckled her harness, the dark shadows dove toward her. She ducked when they sliced the lines connecting her canopy to her harness, thankfully missing her. The wind caught the fabric and it flew off.

The shadows dropped to the ground, each forming a black-eyed coyote the size of a small horse.

*Isn't* this *fun.*

The coyotes spread out, growling. Another gust of wind took the paraglider canopy over the edge.

Shay sighed. "So much for getting off this rock the easy way. Whatever."

The tomb raider pulled out her 9mm and put two rounds into the first coyote, which collapsed and sizzled.

*Okay, didn't expect that.*

She jumped to the side as another one leapt. The animal let out a howl as it fell over the edge to the waiting ground far below.

The remaining coyote charged Shay and she squeezed off three shots before the animal reached her. Blood splattered its gray fur.

Shay hissed as the huge mass of muscle slammed into her, knocking her to the hard ground. Her gun flew from her grip and landed close to the edge, so she went for one of her adamantine knives, but the dying shadow coyote didn't move.

The body sizzled and slowly started to disintegrate into smoke. The tomb raider pushed what was left of the corpse to the side.

"That was close."

Shay retrieved her gun and holstered it. Moment like this would be nice to have a partner. Not yet, though. Lily wasn't ready, even if she was itching to go.

Peyton was barely able to contain her in the warehouse with things to do. Shay thought about introducing her to the library warehouse but no one knew of her private sanctum and for now, she was going to keep it that way.

Soon there was nothing left of the two bodies but a cloud of thick black smoke that floated above her.

She didn't know how the magic used to summon the coyotes worked but didn't care since bullets and falling hundreds of feet killed them. Sometimes the fine details were just a distraction. Plus, them being visible was handy.

Shay shook her head and walked to the edge of the mesa. The wind rushed past her as she leaned over and surveyed the area. The shrub- and tree-covered ground lay hundreds of feet beneath her. Four intimidating buttes surrounded her, but there was no sign of any magical portal.

The only sign of magic was the cloud of black smoke drifting from near some trees, confirmation of the fatal fall for the shadow coyote.

"Damn it! This is the place. It has to be."

Shay's phone still refused to power on, and she stared down at the spinning compass in her other hand.

She snorted. "So much for the backup plan."

Tomb raids were a lot like hits—sometimes the job didn't go according to plan, but a professional didn't whine. At least, they didn't whine too much. If she couldn't handle a few inconveniences here and there, she might as well get an office job.

Shay snickered at the thought of sitting in some office pushing paperwork. She'd last about two days before she shoved some asshole's face into a toilet or HR received complaints about her foul mouth.

"I keep pulling people off the street, I'm going to need my own HR."

More coyotes howled in the distance, and the tomb raider gritted her teeth. She'd thought she'd have more time to find the entrance to the Cueva de Niza, but the dark reinforcements were already closing on her. If they hadn't known where she was before, the clouds of their buddies' smoke was a dead giveaway. Nice, that.

"Guess the AR goggles are pointless with all this interference," she muttered.

She recalled the translation from her notes.

*Come from the sky to stand in the center of the mesa between the four buttes. Look to the north, then walk to the edge. Turn then to the east and walk to the edge. Turn then to the south and walk to the edge.*

*You must walk this exact path. Once you reach the final edge, prove your courage. You must jump. The cave is watching. Those who refuse risk will be denied entrance for their cowardice.*

Shay moved to the center of the mesa and followed the directions. When she reached the final edge, she fished a grappling hook connected to nylon rope out of her backpack.

She took a deep breath and secured the hook on an outcropping near the edge.

"Here goes nothing."

The tomb raider leapt off the edge and plummeted toward the ground. Her rope caught and jerked her and she dangled there for a moment, but there was still no sign of the portal.

"Why can't this shit ever be easy?"

Shay climbed up the rope and pulled herself back onto the mesa.

More howls ripped through the desert air, this time closer.

She unfastened her hook and coiled her rope. A smile popped onto her face.

Where there was nothing before, now the air near the edge of mesa glowed with a faint lavender.

At least she'd confirmed the portal's location. That left one possible solution for getting through it—one she didn't like at all.

"Fuck, this is stupid."

Shay moved closer to the edge, still gripping her hook. She sighed. Just because she had to risk her life by throwing herself off the edge of the mesa didn't mean she had to be a complete fucking idiot about it. Well, no more of an idiot than anyone who jumped from hundreds of feet up.

The cave was watching, or so the translation said. The question remained how much the damned cave understood what it saw.

"Okay, attempt number two."

She leapt off the edge and resisted the urge to close her eyes. A few seconds later, a cocoon of warm and humid darkness surrounded her. The darkness gave way to flickering torchlight, and she landed with a thud against hard-packed earth.

"Damn it!"

Shay winced and rubbed her butt before looking around.

The cave was so large she could barely see the other side and torches circled the walls. Stone pillars stretching to the ceiling filled the chamber, several inscribed with the Seal of Solomon.

The shadow coyotes didn't seem like the kind of creature or spirit that would be summoned with that kind of magical symbol, but Shay was a tomb raider, not a witch.

She reloaded her gun and stepped toward the glinting pile of turquoise and gold lying in the center of the chamber. She frowned as she looked at the treasure.

Her target, the Ring of de Niza, wasn't anywhere obvious. Digging through a pile of gold and turquoise would be far less fun than it sounded, especially when her enemies were close.

Something buzzed behind her and Shay spun, her gun raised.

A huge coyote appeared after a bright lavender flash ten feet above the ground and the snarling beast landed on all fours. Two more arrived a few seconds later and they all charged, growling.

Shay cleared her magazine into their bodies and reloaded as the animals disappeared into smoke.

Her breathing ragged, she stood rigidly, her gun pointed at the entrance. She waited for a couple of minutes, heart thumping, but no other coyotes arrived.

*They know where I am. Shit. Need to hurry this crap up.*

Shay's immediate worry disappeared with a dark snicker. It didn't matter in the end. She wouldn't be able to escape the cave without the ring anyway.

"Guess it's time to start pawing my way through some treasure."

---

Finding the ring didn't take as long as Shay expected, but it still took longer than she wanted. The simple turquoise ring with a silver band didn't look like much, but it would net her two million dollars when she handed it to the client.

Shay took a deep breath. She'd committed the activation phrase to memory and practiced. An easy task usually, but not so simple when it was in an archaic language.

She slipped on the ring.

"Let this ring bind this spot to the next under the watchful gaze of Raphael," she chanted in Old Castilian.

A wave of heat shot through Shay's body, followed by a chill to her very bones. She collapsed to her knees and closed her eyes, and after a long moment, a familiar warmth encompassed her.

Shay opened her eyes. She was back in the center of the mesa, but a pale man in a safari hat standing a few yards away kept her from sighing in relief. His fingers grasped a thin onyx wand, and a faint black energy field hovered in front of him.

He smiled. "Excellent. I didn't want to risk going in, but the fact you're here shows that you've found it."

Glad she hadn't holstered her gun, Shay fired at him, but the bullets burst into smoke as they hit the energy field. She kept pulling the trigger until her gun clicked empty.

The man coughed. "It's rather smoky, don't you think?"

"Fuck you, asshole."

"I wish to applaud your bravery, Aletheia."

Shay chuckled to herself. At least the asshole only knew her alias. "So, you're Coyote Boy?"

The man tapped his wand against his forehead. "Something I learned a long time ago. Sometimes it's easier to draw from the patterns already inherent to an area."

"They weren't so tough. Just took a few bullets."

"True, but they kept you busy." He shrugged. "And now I'm here."

"Why didn't the defensive spell on the mesa force you to jump down there?"

The man grinned. "Who says I didn't? You'd be surprised at the kind of tricks I can pull off with my magic." He shrugged. "Now, I'm not an unreasonable man. I've no desire to kill a woman as beautiful and resourceful as you."

Shay snorted. "Could have fooled me. Your damn coyotes have been hounding me since Sedona."

"They have, but you survived, didn't you? You've proven you're worthy of being spared, and I'm willing to grant clemency in this case."

"How nice of you."

The man opened his free hand and gestured. "Give me the ring, and you walk away. You can't even appreciate the true power of that ring. It's worthless to someone like you."

"Actually, it's worth two million dollars."

He laughed. "Ah, of course. After all, you do this for love of money."

"Something like that, but I doubt you want this ring to help save orphans or some shit."

"That's true." The man's smile vanished. "Hand it over, or you die here in the middle of the desert and no one will ever find your body. You'll serve no other purpose than feeding scavengers."

"I've got another suggestion."

"What's that?"

Shay charged as she reached for one of her knives. He laughed. She slashed with her knife, but her attack was stopped cold as if she'd smashed the weapon into a brick wall.

The man arched a brow. "It didn't disintegrate. Interesting. Apparently, you do keep a few magic toys around after all. Alas, not enough, tomb raider."

"They're specially made, asshole."

The tomb raider backed away, her knife still up. Her adamantine knives might be able to withstand his magic, but she doubted her fists or feet could.

A grin spread over her face when she noticed something.

He shook his head. "You're an eager one, aren't you? I salute you, Aletheia. I'll remember you fondly once you're dead."

Shay flung a frag grenade at him.

The man rolled his eyes, but his nonchalance changed to wide-eyed terror once he realized she'd not thrown it directly *at* him but *over* him. The wizard looked up at the grenade just in time for the explosion. His field remained in front of him, but there was no sign of it at his back.

Shay took her chance and rushed the man without a word, yell, or even a grunt and slammed her knife into his exposed back. He cried out and dropped his wand, and the tomb raider finished the job by slitting his throat.

The man collapsed to the ground.

Shay sighed and shook her head. "Still have to climb down. That's annoying."

## 4

"Y̲ou've got to be shitting me." Shay laughed into her phone. "Boner pills?"

Peyton chuckled on the other end. "Boner *powder*, but yeah. Magical aphrodisiac. I don't know all the details, but it requires a crap-ton of Oriceran ingredients, and the client is willing to pay fifty thousand for you just to pick it up and hold on to until you can hand it to a courier. Hey, put that down!"

Shay could hear Lily yelling, "Whatever."

"Things going alright back at the ranch?"

"Some people have to touch everything. One of these days, that's going to have negative consequences," he yelled, holding the phone away from his mouth.

"Talk to me about the job, Peyton. This sounds too good to be true. This asshole expecting someone to come after it?"

"Nope," Peyton offered. "And I've poked around to confirm that. To be honest, I think the reason he needs you is kind of...well, gross."

"Gross?"

"Well, semi-gross." Peyton cleared his throat. "From what I can find out, the power of the magic is enhanced if it's kept close to a 'beautiful female of strong will' for at least a day."

Shay barked a laugh. "And how does this guy even know what I look like?"

"I really played up how Aletheia is as beautiful as she is wise and all that." He snickered. "Look, it's an easy fifty thousand. If this is just about some horny old man thinking a hot chick's going to enhance his boner powder, I don't see the problem."

"I didn't say there was a problem, just wanted to know. Okay. I've got to head to Virginia to help Brownstone drop Alison off, so I'll grab the case before that and drop it off when I come back. Easiest job I've had in a while—as long as I don't think about it too much."

Shay found the whole thing more amusing than anything else. Some things would always remain the same, no matter how the world changed.

"Okay," Peyton replied. "I'll contact the client and get a pick-up schedule."

"Teach Lily what you can while I'm gone and take her to my gym to box. I've set it all up with the manager."

"She's already figured out my computer system. Girl has a crazy brain."

"She's a gray elf. I hear it comes with the territory."

"Yeah, well take her with you on one of these before she learns my job. I don't have a plan B. Did you know how much she could eat before you brought her home for keeps?"

"Bye Peyton."

---

Shay leaned her back against the wall of the abandoned warehouse waiting for the arrival of the courier. The buzz of a Peyton-controlled drone circling the air helped keep the tension out of her body. No one would surprise her.

Shay couldn't decide if this was the best or worst job she'd ever taken. It'd be easy money, that was for sure, but that assumed it didn't involve some incubus showing up and trying to take her soul.

*Yeah, like to see one of those assholes try.*

She grinned to herself.

"There's a car coming," Peyton reported through her earpiece.

"Anything suspicious? Any additional movement in the area?"

"Nope. Why should there be? Did you see something?"

"Nah. The job's just too easy."

Peyton chuckled. "Not really. The problem with a lot of people is, they might want to sell it."

Shay gritted her teeth. "If some magic douche shows up I'm gonna be pissed off."

"I've checked into the job. This time every corner, I swear. You've checked into the job. It is what is. Sometimes things *are* what they appear. You've got a rep now, so people are willing to pay a little more for things like this." He laughed. "Maybe you should stop tomb raiding and become a courier."

"No way in hell. You know the problem with being a courier?"

"No, what?"

"With tomb raiding, there's a chance you might *not* be targeted. When you're a courier, the chance is high that you will, especially with the high-end shit. Otherwise, they'd just mail it."

"If you say so. You wouldn't have to travel so much."

"I like traveling."

A black sedan turned the corner, and Shay reached inside her jacket to rest her hand on her pistol's grip.

The sedan pulled to a stop and a man stepped out of the car, briefcase in hand.

He cleared his throat. "Please confirm who you are."

"Aletheia. 'Colorless green ideas sleep furiously.'"

The man nodded, satisfied at the passphrase, and held out the briefcase. "You'll need to keep it for at least twenty-four hours. It'll need to be within twenty feet of you for at least twelve of those hours. The more time you spend around it, the greater the chance the client will grant a bonus."

Shay saluted. "Don't worry. I'm sure he'll be able to get it up soon enough."

The other man frowned. She shrugged and offered him a smile.

*Time to see how much Brownstone trusts me.*

Shay sat in silence as Brownstone drove them to his church in his F-350. Alison sat in the back with her hands in her lap.

Now that the tomb raider was two million dollars richer, she could afford a day or two off to help Brownstone take Alison to her new school. The idea of heading into an entire school filled with magic users didn't do wonders for Shay's paranoia, but she reminded herself it wasn't like the School of Necessary Magic would be filled with the kind of people she ran into on tomb raids.

"This won't take long," Brownstone assured them as he pulled up in front of the church. "Just have to talk to Father McCartney for a quick moment."

"I'm fine. Not going into a church," Shay muttered. The last thing she needed was any Catholic guilt.

Alison sighed. "I wonder what kind of religion my mom believed in."

Shay and Brownstone both looked at the girl.

Even now Alison looked normal enough, the only visible hint of her otherworldly heritage the natural white ends on her dark hair, but she wasn't a normal girl. She was a half-Drow princess with a powerful magical heritage who could see people's souls and the energy from magic.

"Maybe that's something you can find out at the school," Shay suggested. "There are Oricerans there. Some of them might be as old as your mom was."

Her mother's massacre of the Grayson mercenaries had proven just how dangerous a Drow could be. Shay and Brownstone were lethal, but Alison's mother had killed scores of men while close to death.

A good killer always recognized the killing talents of another. Brownstone could kick a lot of ass and she respected him for that, but even *he* would have to be careful around a Drow based on what they'd seen.

Alison smiled, oblivious to the lethal thoughts running through Shay's head. "I hadn't thought of it that way."

Shay still hadn't told Brownstone about Lily. There was time and things were complicated enough. Better to see if Lily was even going to last. Besides, Shay had spent a lifetime taking care of her own business. Some habits would be a little harder to bend, much less break.

Brownstone patted the girl on the shoulder and stepped out of his truck.

Shay waited until the bounty hunter had stepped into the church to speak. "He's done a lot of research about the school. So have I."

Alison smiled. "I know. It's just a lot of changes. I was living with my mom and dad, and now Mr. Brownstone is looking after me, and I'm going off to a magic school. I know it'll be good for me, but I'm still a little scared."

"I think the scariest parts are over. You've been through a lot, and you're strong, to not have let it take you down."

"Was it hard for you to leave home?"

Shay chuckled. "Nah, I didn't like my parents. I was doing my own thing around your age too, but I didn't get to go to a fancy school or anything."

"You turned out all right."

Shay laughed. "That's a matter of opinion, but I'm glad you think so."

Alison let out a contented sigh. "Then I'll try and concentrate on all the cool stuff that's going to happen at the school. It'll be an adventure! And they'll be a lot of kids with magic so I won't be weird or strange."

"Exactly."

Shay resisted a snort at the domesticity.

Soon, she'd be flying with Brownstone to Virginia to drop the girl off.

*How the hell had this happened?*

---

The flight from LAX to Richmond International had gone smoothly enough, and finally they had reached the school.

They pulled into a side road and drove for a few moments, until finally an elaborate wrought iron fence with a gate in the middle blocked their way.

Brownstone slowed the SUV as they approached the fence, looking for some sort of security guard, and drove up to the gate. "They didn't say anything about who to call. I assumed there'd be someone here."

Shay laughed. "Maybe it'll magically know who we are."

The gates swung open as if pushed by invisible forces. No obvious mechanism was visible.

*Magic after all, huh?* Shay thought.

Several minutes later he parked in a circular drive surrounding an elaborate fountain resembling a burning phoenix. Shay helped Alison grab her single suitcase from the back and they headed toward the front of the main building, a Georgian-style mansion—or so Shay informed him.

They were intercepted by an older woman who called, "You must be Mr. Brownstone." She smiled at the teen. "And Alison."

"Am I...supposed to bow or something?" James asked.

Shay slapped a hand to her forehead, rolling her eyes. "Seriously, Brownstone?"

The woman laughed and extended her hand. "How about I just offer you my hand? I'm Eleanor Hudson. I teach magical history and basic spells here."

They spoke for a while longer and finally the woman said, "Well, I do hate to be rude, but I'd like to get Alison's orientation started. In the beginning, many things about the school may be overwhelming to new arrivals, so the orientation is critical to integration."

After James and Alison had finished their goodbyes and Alison had left, Shay turned away and put her hand to her face.

"Problem, Shay?"

She snorted and turned back around, eyes slightly red. "Just the pollen in these Virginian trees."

Brownstone nodded but wisely remained silent.

"C'mon, Brownstone," Shay urged. "We still have a flight back to LA to catch."

## 5

They were supposed to be on their way back to the airport. Instead, they ended up back in a parking spot.

"Problem, Brownstone?"

"We should check the place out more," he rumbled. "To make sure it's safe."

Shay chuckled. "And what...verify that their griffin riders all have their licenses up to date?"

"They have griffins? Kids shouldn't fly around on monsters."

"I don't know. Just saying." Shay shrugged. "Probably. But what else? Gonna inspect some wands to make sure they are UL compliant?"

The bounty hunter grunted. "It wouldn't hurt to look around a little more."

Shay sighed. "No, it wouldn't."

They stepped out of the SUV and made their way toward a sidewalk. The density of students was decreasing.

Shay tried to wrap her mind around Brownstone's

paternalism. The truth was, he didn't know Alison that well, but he'd thrown himself into making sure the girl had a bright future. Killing the Harriken might have started because of revenge, but it'd become something more.

It wasn't like he *needed* to take care of the girl. He could have sent her into the system and let the government worry about it. He owed nothing to her mother.

But the man's only concern seemed to be if he was good enough to help raise Alison, not if he *should*. The guy blathered on about keeping his life simple, but was now a foster parent to a half-Oriceran girl and holding onto a magical wish for her. That shit was many things, but simple wasn't one of them.

*What's going on in your head, Brownstone? Geez, Carson, you should wonder. You've taken in a powerful gray elf who bested an Ice Witch and left her alone with Peyton. Who's crazy now?*

He pointed toward the road leading away from the circle drive. "That gate was a joke. I could climb it in seconds."

"Yeah, except for the whole magic blocking-spell deal. It probably fries people or summons a dragon if they touch it."

He grunted. "And the forest? You could hide a whole group of mercenaries in there."

Shay laughed. "Yeah, and they probably have werewolves and jabberwockies in there, too, if not ferret archers."

Brownstone shook his head. "No security's perfect, not even in a government-sponsored magic school."

"Not saying it is. I'm just saying you shouldn't expect

some sort of military-base layout at a school. At least here, there's a bunch of people with magic and magical creatures. Short of sticking her in Fort Knox or the White House, I don't see how she's gonna be much safer."

Brownstone nodded as they made their way to a narrower path leading between two of the smaller buildings. "You really think it's safe?"

"Yeah, I do. We both did our research. Besides, it's not like LA was kind to her, and if anyone outside this school knew her true heritage and what that meant, they might come for her. At least here she has all these wizards and witches to defend her."

Brownstone frowned and nodded slowly. "Let's just check things out a little more. Maybe I'll find something all the wizards and witches didn't think of."

Shay chuckled. "No problem."

Nothing wrong with an overprotective father. She could respect that, even if she hadn't personally experienced it. The tomb raider's smile faded, and she looked the opposite way.

Respecting Brownstone for parental skills didn't make any sense. They wouldn't help him take down his enemies or gather useful information. It wasn't all that long ago she wouldn't have cared about something like that, and would have considered him weak for caring about some girl he hadn't known for that long.

But there it was—she *did* care.

She shouldn't. Getting too entangled with Brownstone wasn't in her plans, but she couldn't deny her growing respect for the man.

The trip around the school satisfied Brownstone that Harriken assassins wouldn't be emerging from the trees anytime soon, but he kept frowning as they made their way back to the SUV and didn't open his mouth as they started on their way back to the airport.

They were halfway back to the airport before he spoke again, which made things easier for her.

"What's with the case?" Brownstone rumbled.

"Huh?"

"That silver case." He jerked a thumb over his shoulder. "The one in the back."

"Oh, that? Just something I picked up on a quick day job."

They talked about the contents and the job for a minute and Brownstone shrugged. "I half-ass trust you."

"Fair enough."

He exhaled slowly. "Speaking of jobs, I kind of need your help."

After he explained, Shay grinned. "Oh. Well, if someone is paying me, of *course* I'd be glad to help."

"I never doubted it."

Shay pulled out her phone and texted Brownstone.

**I'm on my way to the front now.**

**You find your guy?**

**Yep. I'm richer now for no real effort.**

It felt good to be back in LA and great to be $50k

richer. The courier'd picked up the suitcase, and now Shay could relax until it was time for whatever job Smite-Williams had cooked up for the pair.

Shay navigated through the crowds, her gaze flicking from person to person. She could never be sure who might be in an airport waiting to ambush her, or Brownstone for that matter.

His big-ass F-350 sat outside in the loading zone. She shook her head and couldn't understand what he saw in that relic.

She threw open the door and hopped into the passenger seat.

"Feels good to be in a real vehicle," Brownstone said, flexing his fingers on the steering wheel.

Shay laughed. "I love my Spider, but not enough to marry it—unlike you and this fucking antique truck." She gestured with a flourish. "I now pronounce you man and truck."

"Quality never goes out of style, Shay."

The bounty hunter's phone beeped inside the console. He pulled it out and frowned.

"What?" Shay said.

"The Professor says he got our message, but he doesn't want to meet tonight. He says you should call him, though, for some background info."

Since he looked worried, she spent a few moments reassuring him. Finally she agreed to contact the man. "I'll let you know if he tells me anything useful when I call him."

She still needed some details anyway.

Brownstone nodded.

Shay settled on her couch before calling Dr. Smite-Williams.

"Good evening, Miz Carson."

After the usual pleasantries had been exchanged, he got down to it. "Have you heard of the Green Dragon Crescent Blade?"

Shay agreed that she had and told him what she knew.

Smite-Williams clapped. "Congratulations, Miz Carson. You're very well-informed."

"So that's what you want me to get? That blade, or the jade?"

"Aye, and soon. Within the next few weeks."

They agreed on a price and Shay sighed as the called ended. More than a few of her kind had gone looking for the Green Dragon Crescent Blade, and none had ever come back alive. Some claimed the blade would destroy anyone who lacked the spiritual strength to wield it.

Shay would need help with this one. Unlike academics, she had a variety of colorful contacts and she would call around until she got what she needed.

First, though, she had a lot of research to do.

# 6

---

She shimmied and bounced to the rhythm with abandon, dancing with her girls. It'd been a long time since she'd felt so free.

Some old friends had talked her into going out for the first time in a long time. She had avoided them because she didn't want to discuss her new career, but they'd finally convinced her she needed a night out.

Bella leaned close to Shay's ear. "I think I need a break."

After they'd reached the small table in the corner their friends were holding for them, Kara smiled at them all. "I have a little surprise."

"I've got a new guy," she caroled.

After they had heard every detail, Janelle sighed and shook her head. "I didn't want to bring y'all down, but I kicked my man to the curb yesterday."

"What happened?" Shay asked.

"Darius cheated on me." Janelle pasted on a fake smile.

Shay leaned closer and lowered her voice, her eyes piercing. "I could go kick his ass.

Janelle laughed. "Oh, girl, you're too much sometimes. Imagine little ol' you going after Darius?"

She continued her litany of woe, and Shay reached her limit of bonding. She stood to leave and hugged each of them. "Thanks for all the fun, girls."

"Don't let those bastards at the university work you too hard," Bella suggested with a wink.

"I won't."

Shay's playtime was over. Tomorrow she needed to start her search for the Green Dragon Crescent Blade.

---

Having been a professional killer, Shay never relaxed whenever she was in a dark area where she could find herself in a potential ambush. She couldn't help but think about how *she* might kill someone in a place like that.

When she spotted the man lingering suspiciously in the parking lot, she focused on him. After a few more steps she realized he was standing near Janelle's car.

*Wait, is that Darius?*

She'd never met the man, but she'd seen plenty of pictures. Given everything Janelle had just said, there was zero reason for the man to be hanging out in the parking lot waiting for her.

*Yeah, this isn't good.*

Shay's friend's phone had beeped a few times over the night, but no one had paid attention to it since it was girls' night. It wasn't like they all didn't get a lot of messages. Even Shay had gotten a lot from Peyton, not that she would tell her girls who'd sent them.

The tomb raider sighed and altered her course. She'd offered to handle boyfriend trouble earlier, so she might as well follow up on it.

"Hey, Darius," she called.

The huge man turned toward her with a frown on his face. "I don't know you. Get out of my face. I'm waiting for my girlfriend."

Shay rolled her eyes. "That's the thing. You might not know me, but *I* know *you*, and I know Janelle's done with you."

His lips curled into a sneer. "She's not done with me until I *say* she's done with me. Oh, so you're one of her whore friends? You're the ones filling her head with bullshit about being independent and strong? That why she hasn't been answering me?"

"Leave now, asshole. Leave Janelle alone and stop calling her."

"She didn't block me. That means she wants to hear from me. She owes me anyway for putting up with her." He patted his chest.

Shay snorted. "Listen to yourself. *You're* the cheater, not her."

"Can't blame a man for wandering. It's just our nature. She can't bitch because I'm not a saint."

"Okay, here's the thing…you're gonna turn around and leave right now, or something bad is gonna happen."

The man stepped toward her, glowering. "Maybe I need to teach you some lessons like I taught her."

Shay narrowed her eyes. "You've hit Janelle?"

"All I'm saying is that she needed to be taught some respect. Apparently still does."

"You're lucky she tolerated your abusive ass this long then, asshole. If I'd have known, I would have kicked your ass a long time ago."

Darius lunged at her, and she grabbed his wrist and bent it back, then kicked the back of his knee. He went to the ground, howling in pain.

She maintained her painful wristlock and throat-punched him with her free hand. "Here's how this is gonna go… I'm gonna let you go, and you're gonna hop back in your car and leave. You're gonna lose Janelle's number and never go near her again, because if I catch wind of you sniffing in her direction I'll add your balls to my collection. Understand?"

Tears leaked from the man's eyes, and he nodded as he sucked in air. Shay released his wrist and took a step back, her body still tense.

Darius stumbled to his feet and ran in the opposite direction.

Shay grinned. "Little ol' me took him down just fine."

It'd been a long, fun night, but that didn't make it any less exhausting. It was time for bed.

Shay slipped underneath her covers, humming to herself—and stopped as if she'd heard the Nuevo Gulf Cartel at her door.

*Humming? What the fuck is this? I'm fucking happy?*

Shay shook her head. The idea unsettled her more than facing down an ice witch or some stupid Russian frogmen. Then she relaxed and laughed.

She was *happy*. The unpleasant encounter hadn't erased the great time she'd had with her friends. And that's what they were at this point—actual friends. The same thing went for Brownstone, and even Peyton and Lily. All the evidence pointed in the same direction.

Shay had a real life now—and that meant she had something to lose.

## 7

The trip to Mexico had gone off without too much trouble. She'd needed to make a few stops and check in with a few people, and Brownstone had a hard-on to go after some necromancer bounty later, but they were almost to the location of the artifact.

Light caught Shay's eye, and she slowed the 4Runner before bringing it to a stop. She narrowed her eyes, staring straight ahead.

There were caves in the distance, obscured by dust. The faint semi-translucent shimmer in the air worried her.

"You see that, Brownstone?" Shay inquired.

"Yeah, I see it. Fucking magic."

Shay slowly exhaled. "That must be the cloaking. From what I've read, you can't actually see the caves unless you're already looking for them and generally know where they are. Neat trick."

Brownstone opened his door.

"Stop," Shay called.

The bounty hunter turned to look at her.

"From what I've read, this place might have a lot of traps and shit," Shay explained.

The field archaeologist slammed the driver door shut and took a deep breath, which she held until she passed through the magical field. There was no pain or discomfort, and she was still in her own shape.

She waved and hiked to the entry. Three different caves confronted her now. If she'd had any doubts about being in the right spot, the faded classical Chinese characters carved above the caves erased them. Despite the dry climate, the centuries of wind and dust had taken their toll.

"Seems like the right spot, at least," Shay muttered. "Would be a good time to have Peyton in my ear or even Lily's fifteen minute warning."

The minutes passed as she painstakingly checked each hexagram with the help of an app on her phone. The hexagrams on the first two caves were normal, but over the right-hand cave, she found duplicates of the patterns for radiance and force.

Either the priests had gotten sloppy, or they had been trying to leave a clue that they thought only an educated Taoist priest could decipher.

*Good enough for me*, Shay thought, stepping toward the cave on the right. She pulled out a small flashlight and strapped it to her arm.

"Geez, guys, it's like you moldy old assholes were trying to hide some powerful ancient magical weapon or something."

## 8

The cave narrowed and split off in two directions. No skeletons or traps were obvious in either, so Shay held her breath and listened. A quiet hum and the faint sound of running water reached her ears from one of the paths and she stalked that way slowly, searching for any sign of traps or angry-Taoist-priest ghosts.

*The real trouble was finding the place. I'm already ninety percent to my prize just by being in here and not getting killed by the first trap. I mean, how well could they have fortified this place so far from home?*

Shay's smug satisfaction vanished as her path opened into a large cavern with a huge drop into inky darkness. The sound of running water had increased, swallowing the earlier hum, so she suspected an underground river lay at the bottom of the cavern. She deployed one of the drones she'd brought to check out the terrain ahead.

"Didn't plan on some bitch coming with her fancy flying metal demon, did you?"

A long, curved, bladed polearm lay on the ground. It was clearly a *guandao*. The weapon fit the description of the Green Dragon Crescent Blade.

Shay crept toward it. She wanted to take the whole damn thing. If Brownstone could get his arsenal through Customs, he should be able to get one stupid ancient magical weapon through too.

A distant crack echoed through the cave system. Shay sighed when she realized what she was hearing.

"Oh, Brownstone, who are you shooting at now?"

---

Shay shouldn't have worried. Brownstone's little altercation involved some confused militia members. He hadn't even needed any help.

That didn't stop her from being annoyed.

She had successfully collected the artifact and they *should* have been on their way out of Mexico, but instead he was obsessed with his detour to take down a necromancer. She hadn't minded when he'd first mentioned the job, but when she looked into it she thought the whole thing was a bad idea—not that the bounty hunter listened.

She looked down the path Brownstone had taken. "Hurry up, Brownstone, before I die of boredom and the necromancer has to bring me back."

He knew she wouldn't leave him in the mountains without a way to get back, so now she had to risk her life and the artifact because Brownstone had a raging hard-on for catching the damn necromancer.

Shay sighed. She still had her downloaded messages and emails available, and it wasn't like she'd been keeping up with them since arriving in Mexico. She picked up her phone and started reading.

There were a few emails and texts from her friends talking about the great time they all had dancing the other night. Janelle even commented that Darius hadn't been willing to give up, but suddenly after that night, he stopped calling her. A blessing, she called it.

Shay snickered. "I'd call it more an ass-kicking."

Later that evening Shay sat on the edge of her bed. She couldn't help but chuckle at how the day had unfolded. She'd collected a Chinese artifact in Mexico. Brownstone had fought both humans and the undead, getting himself a nice little necromancer head to turn in for a bounty.

The man was something else. She'd never met someone that powerful who possessed such a strange combination of naivete and cockiness. The bounty hunter got the job done, but she couldn't ignore the strange amulet she'd seen him wear or the odd changes to his eyes during the fight with the Harriken.

The man didn't claim to be Oriceran, but she had a hard time believing that an amulet that made him bulletproof wasn't a magical artifact. Shay's curiosity kept poking at her. She'd need to investigate sooner rather than later.

Brownstone had decided to head back to LA, which made sense. He'd done what he needed, and she'd collected the artifact the Professor wanted in exchange for helping Brownstone.

When she'd called Smite-Williams, he'd mentioned he had some other work for her but there was no hurry.

Her phone rang. It was Peyton.

"Hey, Peyton."

"No, it's me, Lily. I borrowed Peyton's phone." The phone was muffled as Lily said, "Grab for the phone again and lose a finger."

"Play nice, he's necessary to the operation and all of his fingers would make things run more smoothly."

Lily let out a snort. "I can make it around the obstacle course without stopping and I flattened your sparring partner. He said you owe him extra."

"How are you at taking direction?" There was a silence on the phone.

"Getting better at that one."

"I know what you're getting at, and yes, I'll take you out on a job. Soon. But, see if you can take direction from Peyton."

Lily let out a groan and Shay could hear Peyton in the background. "What? What? Has something gone wrong?"

Shay had to suppress a laugh. "If you can follow Peyton's directions without shortcuts then I'll know you're ready."

"That's harder than dangling from the warehouse ceiling, but I'll do it."

"Do what?" asked Peyton. "Give me the phone. Finally! Hey, Shay. Everything still okay?"

"Yeah. I'm still figuring out if I'm gonna stick around Mexico for a day or two."

"You really think that's a good idea? You're in Nuevo Gulf Cartel territory."

Shay snorted. "I'm okay. It's not a big deal."

A distinct meow sounded over the line.

"What the hell was that?" Shay inquired.

"What?"

"That noise."

"What noise?"

Shay groaned. "Are you fucking with me? The meowing noise."

"Don't know what you're talking about."

She rubbed the bridge of her nose. It wasn't worth fighting about.

"You at the warehouse right now, correct?"

Peyton laughed. "Come on. I don't always have to be at the warehouse."

"But I'm on a job, and I might need support."

"You already got the artifact, so you're done with the job. And I don't like working from home."

Shay frowned. "Whatever. Fine. Why did you even call?"

Did Peyton have a cat? Brownstone's experience with pets had convinced Shay they were a bad idea, but she wasn't going to bust Peyton's balls over a cat, especially since he was training Lily and keeping the complaining to a minimum. Then again, hiding the animal was suspicious —unless it wasn't a cat.

"Anyway," Peyton continued, breaking Shay out of her thoughts. "I was just checking on some stuff, and since you're already down there I thought you might want to check into some strange rumors."

"Rumors?"

"Yeah, a lot of buzz on some of the tomb raider forums. There's a small village in the mountains just north of Cabo. Rumor is that a tomb raider disappeared there last week, and he was supposed to have been tracking some big artifact. A lot of people just found out about this today because some of his people are reaching out."

"Huh. What artifact was he tracking?"

Peyton sighed. "No one seems to know. The thing is, people are on the move. If you head out right now, you might be able to find out what's going on and grab it before anyone else shows up. I'm thinking you've got less than a day before other people show up."

"Give me the coordinates and I'll look into it first thing in the morning. Can't hurt to check."

Peyton laughed. "Famous last words."

"Don't worry, I'm on a roll."

---

Shay might respect Brownstone, but she didn't need the man. The morning jaunt to the village would prove that. Scoring an artifact with no client attached would be a major coup.

She had her knives, but otherwise not a lot in the way of personally useful magical weaponry. Given that she was increasingly running into wizards, witches, and strange monsters, she should be better prepared. She needed a magical arsenal as big as her conventional one. That's where Lily might come in handy, too.

The job should be easy. She'd sweep into town, throw

some money around, and get someone to admit where the tomb raider had slunk off to. She wasn't above stealing the artifact from the villagers if they'd stolen it from the tomb raider. This wasn't about the honor of her profession, just risk evaluation.

She chuckled at the thought as she pulled into the village...and slammed on the brakes.

Bodies littered the street, some torn limb from limb. Vultures picked at the corpses, and the state of decay made it obvious they'd been dead for a few days.

"Guess the villagers didn't steal shit from the tomb raider," she muttered.

Shay threw open her door and stepped out. She grabbed her tactical harness from the passenger seat and slipped it on.

Something awful had happened in the village. No, not just something awful—something *supernatural*. Cartel assholes might chop a person's head off, but they didn't rip bodies apart and leave them in the middle of the village. They weren't strong enough for that.

She shook her head. Whatever had happened in the village, it must have gone down fast enough that no one could get out a call for help.

Shay sucked in a breath. A drone survey or an AR goggle sweep might be in order. Given what she'd dealt with in Ohio recently, she couldn't assume that she could spot her enemy without assistance.

No sooner had that thought crossed her mind when a flicker of movement caught her eye. Something human, or at least human-shaped.

*Well, at least I can see it this time.*

Shay pulled out her pistol and headed closer to one of the rows of brightly-painted adobe houses lining the sides of the main dirt road leading through the village. Caution kept a person alive whether it was a normal or a magical fight.

The tomb raider edged to the corner where she'd seen the movement and waited. She counted to three, then spun, her gun raised.

A tall pale bald man stared back at her. Intricate curving patterns had been etched all over his body, made evident by his lack of clothing other than a loose rope belt connected to a large leather pouch. His pointed ears registered after a second.

Shay kept her gun pointed at the elf. "You're gonna tell me what the fuck happened here and you're gonna give me a good answer, or I'm gonna put you down."

The elf stared at her. His eyes were solid black. Not exactly standard, even on his kind.

"Why?" he croaked back. His deep and booming voice was not what she'd expected.

"Because there's a whole fucking village of dead people here, asshole, and you're Suspect Number One."

"All that lives dies. Such is the way of existence. Planets die. Stars die. People are nothing."

Shay snorted. "Well, aren't you just a bag of sunshine? Let me put it this way, asshole—I'm the woman with the gun, and I want answers."

"I've given you your answers."

"Let me rephrase it. Did you kill these people?"

"Yes. I needed their lives. It's been so long. I was so

hungry and overwhelmed that I risked losing my vessel, but I'm calm now."

"Good for you." Shay's face twitched. She doubted it would be more than a couple of minutes before she emptied her gun into the elf.

The scarred elf inhaled deeply. "You smell of magic, and...something else."

Shay blinked. "Since when can elves fucking smell like that?"

"The vessel is unimportant." He tilted his head like a curious bird. "You stink of something else, too. Unfamiliar, yet familiar. How long has it been since I've smelled that?"

"Where's the artifact? In the bag?"

"Artifact?"

"You killed a man here for an artifact, didn't you? Then killed all these people? Ripped some of them apart."

The elf continued to tilt his head from side to side. "I killed them all, but the artifact? Oh, my prison. It's gone now." He patted the pouch. "Other things he had. Interesting things."

"Give me that."

"Ah, I know."

"Know what?"

The elf pointed at Shay. "The stench—it's gnome mixed with just a hint of elf. The smell of gnome is strong. No. You can't have what I hold, She Who Stinks of Gnome. It gives me hints. Places to visit. For the future."

"You know what, fuck this! I've had enough of this shit. Just die already." Shay fired at his head.

Unlike her last encounter, the bullet hit its target. The

elf jerked back and blood sprayed, covering the ground. He straightened, and the wound started closing immediately

Shay emptied her magazine into his body. It shook with each blow, but he didn't so much as grunt in pain.

The elf shook his head. "The vessel is strong." His eyes glowed red. "I will not return, She Who Stinks of Gnome."

The tomb raider holstered her pistol and pulled one of her adamantine knives.

"This what you smell, asshole? I think I've got this figured out." She pointed at him with the knife. "I don't know what the fuck you are, but I think you're wearing that elf like a suit. I'll tear it off you and send you back to whatever freaky place you belong."

"No. You will die. Everything that lives dies."

Shay grinned. "Nope. Here's the thing...you killed everyone here, but you haven't come after me. You know what I think? I think you're fucking afraid, and I think my gnome stink has something to do with that."

The elf stepped toward a wall and punched through it. Chunks of adobe and brick shot from the hole. "You will die."

"Everything that lives dies. That includes you, right, asshole?"

"No. I don't live, I exist. I cannot die."

"Guess we'll put that to the test then, huh?"

The village was dominated by low walls forming lots of narrow passageways between the homes, and a lot of flat roofs. This could work. Fighting this possessed elf or whatever the fuck he was wasn't high on Shay's list of favorite things, but she wanted whatever artifact he had on him.

For that matter, she didn't like the idea that he'd slaughtered a village. If she could help Brownstone get revenge for a dog, she could spare a few minutes to teach some supernatural asshole not to underestimate humanity.

Shay rushed toward the elf, her knife at the ready. He threw a punch, but she dodged to the side. He might be strong, but he was slow—at least at that moment, and she didn't want to wait around for him to get hungry again. She slashed his neck with her blade and took several steps back.

The blood poured from the wound, but the elf didn't go down or even look mildly inconvenienced. It pissed Shay off.

Smugness swallowed the anger when she noticed the wound wasn't closing.

"How that's for gnome stink?" Shay taunted.

The elf bounded toward her and Shay jumped and grabbed the lip of the roof, yanking herself up in time to avoid the iron grip of her enemy. The glowing-eyed elf stepped a few feet back, then leapt into the air.

"Shit, that's one way to do it."

Shay threw the knife at the elf, then ran and hopped onto the next rooftop. She spun to face him and grabbed another knife. No, Lily is not quite ready for this shit.

The elf landed with a thud and the knife sticking out of his chest. He yanked it out and tossed it away. Like her slash to his neck, the new wound didn't close.

A blow to the brain sounded good in theory, but Brownstone's recent experiences with zombies convinced her it was no guarantee of a win. She pulled out her remaining adamantine knife.

The elf jumped again, and Shay sprinted and leapt back to the original roof. She offered her enemy a wink. Nothing like taunting a possessed elf.

He punched through the roof and yanked up a large chunk of adobe and Shay jumped backward off the roof to avoid the makeshift projectile. She rolled into her landing to mitigate the worst of the fall, but knew she'd be feeling it the next day.

Her enemy was already plunging toward her when she stood and brought up both her knives and sliced. The elf's body slammed into her as his head flew in the opposite direction.

She pushed off the headless corpse, surprised she'd managed the decapitation with the knives, but the asshole's downward momentum and the gnome-enhanced sharpness of the blades had helped.

Shay stepped back and waited for the body to rise, but it remained motionless as a pool of blood formed beneath it.

Brownstone had the right idea. Sometimes you just had to behead the motherfucker.

The tomb raider sheathed her knives and recovered the third. They'd proven their worth, and she doubted she'd be able to replace them easily.

Shay jogged back to the body and nudged the pouch with her foot. There was something hard inside, so she opened it.

A smooth polished stone decorated with symbols she didn't recognize lay inside. She shrugged—a little research didn't bother her—and pocketed the artifact.

"I don't know what the fuck *that* was all about," she muttered to herself.

She wasn't sure if she'd finished off her opponent, but she wasn't going to stick around to find out. Besides, it wasn't like there was anyone else he could kill.

———

Shay didn't call Peyton until she was well away from the village. She half-expected the headless body to leap on her 4Runner and didn't want to be distracted. Once the village disappeared behind her, she stopped on the side of the road and pulled the stone from her pocket.

She took a few pictures with her phone and called Peyton.

"Hey, Shay," he answered.

"I'm gonna send you some pictures. I want you to do a little background research for me."

"Pictures of what?"

"The stone I took from whatever the fuck I just killed."

Peyton sighed. "It wasn't just a matter of paying some bribes, then?"

"Nope. Some fucking weird possessed elf. Show Lily, too and see if she recognizes anything or... or anyone."

"Sorry."

"Don't worry. I geared up and expected trouble, so I won. Anyway, check out these pictures and see if you can get me any leads."

"Will do."

Something or someone meowed.

Shay laughed. "Is that a cat or a girl? I can't tell."

"Um, gotta go. I'll let you know about your symbols." Peyton hung up.

Shay stared at her phone and shook her head. She could worry about what he was hiding later. It was probably more embarrassing than dangerous.

She'd find out soon enough. There was no way she was staying in Mexico for another day after that fucked-up encounter.

---

## 9

Shay ran up and down the new stairs she'd added to her obstacle course in Warehouse One, her breathing heavy. There was nothing that killed her jetlag quicker than a good workout. Lily was moving steadily just behind her, easily keeping up. Her movements were getting smoother, and she was less impetuous.

Shay was thinking her newest asset would be ready sooner, rather than later. But start out with something simple, if that even existed. The last job was supposed to be simple and it was anything but...

Shay still had no idea what she'd fought in Mexico, but she doubted it was just an elf. She wasn't an expert on demons, but that was the obvious explanation.

*Guess I should have called in a priest.*

Lily let out a loud grunt and worked her way up the jumping bars. Shay was busy nimbly leaping onto a series of moving, narrow platforms, suspended from guide wires that could swing at the slightest touch. It was taking concentration and quick movements to make it through to the last one and grab onto the sliding pipe.

Lily made it to the top and grabbed onto the Tarzan rope, letting out a yell as she swung across a swath of the warehouse and came to land on a mat.

The tomb raider continued through the rest of the obstacle course, making it to her metal balance beam as she considered the implications of priests fighting demons.

The return of magic was making so many things confusing. Even if people on Earth had made a lot of incorrect assumptions about supernatural beings, it was hard to deny that the people in the past had been onto something. If demons were real, it wasn't that crazy a thought that priests might use magic to deal with them.

Shay took a deep breath as she continued moving through the course to her new final obstacle. Changing things up helped keep her skills fresh, and she'd added it at the same time she'd added the stairs.

She jumped for a suspended bar and swung back and forth a few times to build momentum before leaping over to catch the edge of a wall. After pulling herself up, she climbed down the rope hanging on the other side.

The tomb raider chuckled. The stone still bothered her. She had no idea what it was, which meant she couldn't even think about using or selling it, but it wasn't like she could spend much time digging into it.

Mysteries with no clients didn't pay. That shit could wait. "Come on, Lily, let's go get pizza."

Shay stepped out of her Spider into Warehouse Two, frowning. Almost all the cubicle walls that defined Peyton's makeshift apartment were gone, which somehow made the entire room feel emptier. Lily came around and stood next to her, looking at the empty space.

"Was it something I said?"

It bothered her, and she wasn't sure why. Peyton deserved his own place, even if she thought it was a horrible security risk. He needed to start having some semblance of a normal life again.

"Peyton?" she called.

He didn't answer.

Shay went into the office and sat down at his computer to check what he'd been working on. The security system beeped, and one of the loading bay doors rose.

The lack of blaring alarms told her Peyton was arriving —or he might have been tortured into giving up the codes.

She pulled out her 9mm and stepped out of the office, hoping she wouldn't have to kill anyone in here and be forced to abandon the building. "You hang back," she said as Lily grabbed a tennis racket left behind by Peyton.

One of her black vans pulled in, Peyton at the wheel.

The researcher waited until the bay door closed and hurried out of the vehicle.

"Sorry I'm late."

Shay eyed him. "Traffic that bad?"

"I'd like to say, 'Hey, that's LA for you,' but not so much. It's just that I'm on my fifth route to get here. Can't make a beeline every day. Too much of a pattern, right? Security first."

The tomb raider gave him an approving nod. Security

was a mindset as much as it was a system or set of policies. That didn't change the underlying problem, though.

"You're gonna wear yourself out," Shay observed. "Still think the apartment is worth it?"

Peyton laughed. "Says the woman who has her own place, but yeah, I *do* think it's worth it. It makes me feel like an actual person rather than some weird hermit you keep in this warehouse. No offense, Lily. It's like an initiation into Team Shay."

"None, taken," she said, holding up the tennis racket.

"I've got something to ask you, and I want you to be honest," said Shay.

Peyton's face tightened, and his gaze dropped.

Shay snickered and realized she still had her gun out. She holstered it. "Just being careful, but it's nothing bad. I want to know what's up with the meowing I keep hearing when I call you."

He shrugged, a nervous look on his face. "I've got a cat. It's not a big deal."

"You've got a cat?"

"Yeah, Osiris. He was a stray, but now he's mine. He's a cat. It's not like he can sell me out to my brother."

"Maybe, but you never know anymore."

Peyton rolled his eyes. "He's just a cat, Shay, not some Oriceran or shape-changing magic user."

"You needed an apartment so you could have a pet?"

Peyton shook his head. "No, I've brought him by here. Lily's met him. Like I said, I want my own place. I've been decorating, and…" He sighed. "Besides, what if I meet someone? Where was I was supposed to bring them, here?"

"*Meet* someone?" Shay kept her face neutral even

though she knew exactly what the man was getting at. Of all her sins, needling Peyton was minor.

"You know…a girl."

Shay opened her mouth to probe deeper when a harsh alarm sounded from the office computer.

"What the hell is that?"

Peyton rushed toward the office. "Perfect! It's here."

"Here?"

"Yeah, my delivery."

Shay's hand drifted back toward her holster. "What the fuck is *here*? Who the fuck did you give this address to?"

"Does gun wielding happen a lot around here because if it does I need to get better prepared," said Lily.

"Your weapons work is your weakest area," said Peyton.

"Said the guy whose hand shakes when he holds one."

Shay gritted her teeth. She'd gone from being sorry the place was empty to ready to take down Peyton.

He shrugged. "Relax, it's not a big deal."

"*Not a big deal?* How the fuck is it not a big deal?"

"It's Purity Solutions."

Shay blinked, now more confused than angry. "Huh?" She shook her head. "As in the cleaners and movers?"

Peyton grinned and bobbed his head. "Yep. Once you confirmed they were the real deal, I figured I could use them. I mean, after all, they come, they go, and they forget they were ever here. And they deliver." He tapped on his computer, and the loading bay opened. The world's most nondescript gray van pulled inside.

The tinted windows denied her a view of the drivers, and it took Shay some effort to keep her attention on the vehicle.

*Magic, huh?*

Shay sighed, still unsure if this was a good idea, let alone not a horrible one. "What are they delivering?"

"A pizza oven. The real thing."

"Oh, sweet! Let me see," said Lily.

Shay groaned. "I told you before. There's a lot more to pizza than just having a pizza oven."

Two men in blue uniforms and short-brimmed hats stepped out of the vehicle and threw open the back. They extended a ramp.

"I don't care if its Purity," Shay bitched. "This is still stupid."

The men ignored their argument as they rolled a dolly with a large stone oven off the van.

Peyton whistled. "You guys really do it all."

They set the oven down near the wall, then returned to the van to grab boxes filled with tools and other supplies. Lily was already opening one of the boxes.

Shay took several deep breaths. Part of her wanted to point her gun straight at Peyton's head, but he was right about Purity. If there was one company on the planet that could be trusted with the location of her warehouse, even temporarily, it was them. It wasn't like they didn't already know where she lived.

She waited for the men to finish their delivery and pull out of the warehouse before returning her baleful gaze to Peyton.

"We need to have another talk about security, Peyton."

Peyton held up a finger. "Hold that thought."

"Hold that thought? What the fuck?"

"Got an alert on my way here. I meant to mention it.

Another quick job. Not any sort of ancient underwater crap or evil haunted Walmart. Just go to a place, sneak in, steal something, and sneak out. It's a one-day thing."

Shay could slap him around about security later. "What? Is this more boner magic?"

Peyton snorted. "Nope. Rich guy wants you to fly into Antarctica to grab some seeds from the seed vault."

"Wait, I thought the big seed vault was in Norway?" asked Lily.

"You've been using my computer again when I'm not here. Talk about that later." The researcher shook his head. "That's the more famous and public one. This one is more low-key, probably because they built it on top of a place where certain groups have been storing magic plants for centuries—long before the truth of Oriceran came out. It used to be completely secret, but word got out and now they just try and keep tourists away. The facilities are top-notch, so it's become another global seed vault even for non-magical stuff. They've also got a secret vault there for high-value seeds, and our client wants some specific ones."

"Let me guess—are they magic beans?"

Peyton nodded. "Well, yeah."

"It's funny how some people in the past had a clue about magic, even as they were keeping things away from the rest of us."

"Isn't that always the way?"

"Because humans handle the idea of magic so well," piped Lily.

"Worthy point. Tell me what they do. The beans? Grow a beanstalk that stretches to the sky?"

"Very funny." Peyton shrugged. "He refused to get into

too much detail, but he did warn that if you got them too warm you'd find out, and you'd also lose the rest of your payment. He offered some cryptic comment about pod people. I don't know."

Shay scratched her cheek. "Is this a job we should take?"

She surprised herself with the question.

Peyton blew out a breath. "I don't know, but it's a very nice payday for a small amount of work. The client's already arranged a cover for you and access codes, and I've verified them. I mean, it's not as easy as carrying around a suitcase of boner powder, but it pays a hell of a lot more. He's also got a little artifact to beat some of the magical security that he'll loan you."

"And there are no strange evil magical penguins waiting for me down there or some shit like that?"

"Nope. Like I said, it's not even a secret place anymore, not in the way it used to be. You'd be traveling down with a group of scientists who are doing research. People won't have any reason to suspect you. Given the place's history, a lot of people still run experiments—both magical and otherwise—that they don't want to talk about."

"You're saying I can tell people to mind their own damned business and they will?"

"Yeah, basically."

Shay shrugged. "I could hide a lot of weapons in a parka."

"You won't even need any. That's how well set up this job is."

"Just when I think I don't need any guns or knives, some asshole shows up with a machine gun and takes me down."

Peyton laughed. "Just saying, but that doesn't change the fact that I already set up all your equipment in Warehouse Three. That was the other reason I was late." He pointed at himself and smiled. "See? Efficient. I know what I'm doing."

"Fuck it, at least this way I can say I've traveled to every continent."

"Take me with you. Peyton's already said this one's easy. It's in the middle of bumfuck nowhere and it's *icy*. As in cold as a witch's… Just in case, take me with you."

She hesitated for a moment. Why the hell not? She was going to have to field test Lily eventually if this experiment was going to get any traction. Hell, would Brownstone take a teenager out in the field? No, probably not but Shay was going to give it a try. Different ideas of parenting.

"Get the gear you've been practicing packing. Give her an ear piece, Peyton. When I get back, there's something I want to show you." Shay pointed at Peyton

"What?

Shay took a deep breath. "Another warehouse."

"You mean there's another one?" Peyton's eyes became saucers, like a kid learning Santa was real.

"You'll see, and I think you'll be pretty damn surprised." Shay winked.

# 10

---

Shay and Lily kept to themselves as the large truck carrying the scientists made its way through the icy wasteland. Shay's transport was at the head of a convoy of three carrying scientists and supplies. A few of the others had tried to talk to them on the plane from Argentina, but Shay staring at them in silence made them shut up. Now they didn't bother trying.

She wasn't worried. It wasn't like anyone expected her or Lily to be chatty, since her cover was a botanist specializing in tropical plants who had been "forced" to go to Antarctica along with a junior assistant. One of Lily's better talents was staring sullenly at strangers.

It was amazing how a few background details could make things less awkward.

The tomb raider admired Peyton's thoroughness in establishing her cover identity in such a short time. The client's information had helped, but the researcher's aid shortened the job from days of prep to simple execution. Annoying deliveries aside, Peyton had proven more useful than she ever could have guessed when she'd decided to save him from the hit.

He'd been a good investment. Hopefully, Lily would turn out to be the same.

Hell, he was even turning into something approaching a good friend.

Shay stared out the window. The endless ice and snow unsettled her. This wasn't a place she'd want to spend a lot of time, but fortunately, they wouldn't need to.

The pilot would be refueling and inspecting his plane, with a planned take-off in about six hours. He expected and was prepared to take a few outgoing staff and deliveries when he departed. All Shay and Lily needed to do after recovering the beans was make it to the plane with a bullshit explanation about how her junior assistant left behind some critical equipment. Once they got back to Argentina, they could take a supersonic flight back to LA with ease.

An easy job, just like the magical Viagra. Shay grinned to herself.

Thirty minutes passed before they arrived at the cluster of low and rugged buildings comprising the World Seed Repository complex. The other scientists chatted among themselves as a huge metal door lifted. The convoy pulled into a garage filled with trucks, both wheeled and tracked, along with several snowmobiles.

The driver cleared his throat. "Welcome to the World Seed Repository. You'll have to badge in one by one. Sorry, that's the policy. The alarm goes off otherwise, and it's a big headache for everyone involved," he muttered under his breath. "You can leave your things here for now."

Everyone opened their doors and filed out of the vehicle. Shay waited until everyone else had gathered their things to step out and collect her backpack, nodding to Lily to follow her as Lily slipped on her own backpack.

The driver shook his head. "You don't need to get that, Doctor."

"I don't go anywhere without my instruments." Shay slipped the backpack over her shoulders.

Shay held her breath and fished out her fake badge. If Peyton or her client had screwed up, things might get messy. She didn't plan to gun down a building full of scientists, but she was also in the middle of Antarctica. Escape might prove logistically more difficult than she was used to. She looked back at Lily to see if she was getting any divination, but the teenager shook her head. Nothing.

*Yeah. Maybe I should be careful about taking jobs to the middle of nowhere?*

She lifted the badge to the security pad...and the light turned green.

*Huh. That was easier than I thought.*

A maze of dull gray hallways confronted them on the other side of the door. She'd memorized their path, but could always grab the downloaded map off her phone if needed. Ten minutes of walking brought them to an elevator.

Shay tapped in the code for the Class-D magic vault and swiped her badge over the security pad. Lily stood with her back to her, keeping watch for anyone who might have gotten an idea to follow them.

The elevator chimed and rumbled down.

The job was so easy she felt like she should be whistling

or humming. The elevator chimed again, and the doors opened into a darkened corridor lined with doors. They made their way halfway down to Vault 67-D.

A gray metal door blocked the entrance. A small computer screen sat to the side, and there was a keypad above the silver and black plaque identifying the door.

After Shay tapped in the code, the door buzzed and the bolt retracted. She spun the heavy metal wheel and pulled open the door. Metal shelves extended back about twenty feet, each holding black boxes with lids.

A blue orb winked into existence in front of them.

Shay held her breath and rubbed the medallion underneath her parka. If the artifact given to her by the client didn't work, she might have to deal with some difficult magical security. The orb circled her for a few seconds before zooming to a stop right in front of the medallion. A second later, it vanished.

"Okay, I guess that's that. Nice."

"This is pretty easy money," said Lily in a hushed voice.

"Yeah, that's when you need to have your guard up the most. Stay close and let me know if you get a vision."

The tomb raider and the gray elf went down the shelves until Shay finally located Box 34.

Shay smiled. She reached into her parka to pull out the medallion and waved it over the box. A series of glowing glyphs appeared and vanished just as quickly. She removed the top without any surprises. It was time to see what was inside.

"What the fuck?" she growled.

"What? What is it?" Lily looked over Shay's shoulder into the box.

Empty. Completely empty.

Shay gritted her teeth. Had the client screwed up? Or Peyton?

Her gaze flicked to the nearby boxes. She had no idea if the medallion would grant her access to them, and searching blindly in a magical vault in a facility filled with people didn't strike her as a good idea.

"Wait right here."

Shay rushed into the hallway to look at the computer screen and tapped a few commands into the pad. Peyton had taught her a few useful commands, but she hadn't thought they would be important. Turned out she was wrong.

The last few lines of the access log displayed.

"Damn it."

According to the log, someone had been in there just minutes before Shay. She might have even passed them in the hallway.

"Fuck, fuck, fuck."

Shay ran back to where Lily was waiting and asked her, "Did you see anyone else?" as Lily shook her head. "Still no vision?"

"It doesn't work in reverse. I never see the past."

"We need to get out of here. Follow me."

Shay closed the vault and they ran toward the elevator. It was too much of a coincidence. There was no fucking way someone had conveniently shown up to the magic vault minutes before her and not taken the beans.

She stood with her teeth gritted the entire way back up. Once clear of the elevator, she sprinted back toward the garage with Lily in tow, her head on a swivel. The kid had good tactical instincts. More than a few passing scientists eyed Shay like she'd gone crazy. Great way to mentor somebody. It is if you're a tomb raider.

Shay burst into the garage and spotted the driver from earlier. The hood of his truck was up, and he was inspecting the engine.

The man looked over at her. "Doctor Calvers?"

"Yeah, yeah. Whatever. Got a question for you."

"Oh, if it's about this, don't worry. Just a routine check."

"No, I have a different question. Has anyone left the facility since we arrived?"

"Just Doctor Petrova. I think that was her name. I don't know, I wasn't her driver. She flew in yesterday."

"Where is she?"

"She took a snowmobile out to inspect some monitoring station." He shrugged.

Shay jogged toward a line of snowmobiles. "I need to talk to her ASAP. We're gonna borrow one of them."

"Oh, you working with her? You know where she is?"

"Yeah, we collaborate at times, and I know the station," Shay lied. She nodded to the closed door. "Can you open that?"

"Sure, one sec." The man pulled out a remote control. He pressed a button, and the massive doors rose, the hum and grinding of metal echoing in the garage.

The tomb raider laughed as she spotted the keys in the vehicle. She hadn't even worried about it, but it made sense. Vehicle theft wasn't high on the list of concerns in a place like this.

Shay mounted the vehicle as Lily got on the back, and

started it, zooming out of the garage before the doors had risen all the way.

"So far, I'm not sure what I've added to this whole thing," Lily yelled from the back.

"It's a first run. No expectations." Besides another kink in the mission.

A fresh trail lay right outside. The mysterious Doctor Petrova might be nothing but another scientist, but she was the only immediate lead the tomb raider had. If it didn't pan out, she was going to have to figure out a different way.

The snowmobile tore through the snow as Lily hung on tight. After a few minutes, Shay realized she was heading right back toward the airport. Her doubts about Petrova being a scientist grew.

*Some bitch took my damned magic beans. But who? Did the client set me up?*

Shay ground her teeth together. A conspiracy was unlikely. It wasn't like this was the first time she'd shown up on a tomb raid when someone else was poking around. She was only surprised that none of their research about the job had caught wind of someone else being interested.

The tomb raider continued to follow the tracks. The dark vehicle and white-clad rider appeared in the distance, but she was closing slowly on them—too slowly. They'd likely hit the airport before she arrived at this rate.

Shay took a deep breath and tried to stop her heart from pounding. She could still salvage this mess. Whoever had grabbed the seeds couldn't just hop on a plane and take off, which meant she still had hours to get the beans from them—by violence if necessary.

The radar tower of the airstrip rose in the distance. The snowmobile ahead suddenly stopped, and Shay frowned. She continued driving toward the person and cut the throttle as she closed, stopping when there was still a good ten yards between them.

The person dismounted. Their thick parka and goggles blocked their face.

"Doctor Petrova?" Shay called. She wasn't going to gun down some random scientist without proof the woman had stolen her beans.

"Ah, that explains it." The response was female, cold, and Russian-accented. If the woman was a fake, at least she was Russian. Something about the voice was familiar, though.

"Explains what?"

The other woman pulled up her goggles. A familiar face, Yulia Solokova—Snegurka the Ice Witch. A jagged scar ran across her left cheek, likely a memento of Shay's last encounter with the woman.

"Huh, you're not dead." Shay unzipped her parka. She was going to need her gun. She could feel Lily's arms tense.

"No. I'm not." A blue crystal wand dropped from her parka's sleeve into her right hand. "It's funny that we should run into each other like this. Very funny."

"I'm guessing you took my beans."

"They aren't yours, now, are they? And you brought a playmate. Who is that with you?" The Ice Witch tried to get a better look but Shay was blocking her line of sight to Lily. Save that surprise for just a moment.

Shay shrugged her left shoulder. Her right hand rested

on her pistol. "You could hand them over. We don't have to do this. It's nothing personal, you know. Just the job."

"I could say the same, Aletheia."

The tomb raider narrowed her eyes.

Yulia nodded. "Yes, maybe I know not who you truly are, but I know what you are, tomb raider." She ran the tip of her wand over her scar. "I don't even begrudge you this. It was an important lesson in overconfidence."

"Why are you even here?"

"To get the beans, of course."

"You're a mercenary guard, though. Who the fuck are you guarding?"

Yulia smiled. "I'm many things." She laughed. "But this is pointless. Don't you realize the situation you're in?"

"What situation? It's not like I'm unarmed."

"No, I wouldn't imagine you'd be that short-sighted, but you really think you're going to take down an Ice Witch in the middle of the land of snow and ice?" The witch sighed. "Foolish." She snapped her wand up and shouted something in Russian. Six blue stones shot from the ice in front of the wand. A blue hexagonal pattern appeared.

Lily suddenly lurched forward and yelled, "Duck," in Shay's ear.

Shay and Lily dropped behind the snowmobile. Shay knew how this show ended. Lily's vision kicked in to save them from the ice spear that hit where Shay had stood. Shay opened up with her pistol, but each bullet fell to the ground encased in ice.

"Damn it."

Preparation meant different things to different people. Shay assumed that being prepared for the milk-run job would involve just bringing her gun and her knives. Now she wished she had a few grenades or a pit to blow the witch into like she had on Oak Island.

Still, she had brought Lily.

*Have to close on her. If my knives can win against that possessed elf, they can help me against Yulia.*

An icy arm rose from the snow right beside Shay and smacked her, sending her sprawling but not before Lily got off a shot of her own, grazing the Ice Witch. A look of recognition came over the Ice Witch's face followed by a sneer.

"This is going to be more fun than I thought. Two birds, one icicle."

Shay rolled to her side. A thick wall of ice shot in front of her. She fired, but her bullet didn't penetrate. Three other walls shot up encasing her. A good jump would get her over the top, but there was no way she could accomplish it without the Ice Witch blasting her.

"Fuck." Shay glared at the Ice Witch through the ice keeping her gaze fixed on her. Less chance the Witch would notice that Lily had seen it all coming and was in position. The teenager fired off another shot, the bullet passing through the Ice Witch's thigh.

She let out a surprised yelp and spun around, her wand in the air, an icicle already on its way at Lily. Lily neatly slid underneath it but not before a rising wall of ice knocked her in the head, her body slamming against a second wall, leaving her unconscious on the ground.

Shay beat her fists against the ice wall, leaving spidery cracks down the sides.

Yulia stepped forward, smiling, but her breathing was

ragged, and her hand was pressed against her thigh. She flourished her wand. "As I said, you have no chance. You were lucky in Canada, but here the entire land is my plaything. You were doomed the minute you decided to follow me." She turned toward her snowmobile, glancing over at Lily and raising her wand.

Shay yelled out quickly, doing her best to taunt the Ice Witch and draw her attention. "Aren't you going to finish me off? I'll be honest—it's not like I'd spare you in the same situation."

"No, you will live for now. Continue to live in your humiliation, Aletheia, knowing that you've been defeated and failed your client." The witch snickered. "Vengeance is pointless if the other person doesn't suffer first. But don't worry, I'm not going to make this easy. After you've suffered enough, then and only then will you die. I'll even leave this little pest for later, if she's even still alive."

The witch pointed her wand at Shay's snowmobile and blue stones floated in front of it. This time, several nested hexagonal blue patterns winked into existence. Ice coated the snowmobile for several seconds and finally formed an almost solid block.

Yulia waved and hopped on her own vehicle. She drove away laughing.

"You should have killed me, bitch. This isn't over." Shay took several deep breaths and ran toward one of the ice walls. She pushed off and leapt, using the momentum to carry her up to the top, freeing herself from her ice prison.

Her elation was short-lived. She ran to Lily and dropped to her knees, feeling for a pulse. She was still alive.

She gently shook the teenager till she opened her eyes and helped her sit up.

"We're in a situation." Shay didn't have a chisel or hammer to free her snowmobile, and even if she had, the witch had probably killed the vehicle.

Lily tried to sit up but cried out in pain, holding her arm in front of her. "I think it's broken," she said between clenched teeth.

"I shouldn't have brought you."

"Fuck that, I'm not complaining." Lily winced and squeezed her eyes shut. "Do you have something I can use for a sling?"

Shay pulled off her scarf and tied it around Lily's neck, helping her ease her arm into the makeshift sling. Lily blinked back tears and let Shay help her to her feet. "Most fun I've had in a long time and still better than living in the pipe."

"That is really saying something, kid. You will make a great tomb raider."

Lily smiled despite the pain and leaned on Shay as they started walking. At least Shay could see the airport in the distance and wouldn't die in the middle of Antarctica.

*Eh. Lily has a point. Still better than bleeding out in my kitchen.*

An hour passed as Shay and Lily trudged toward the airport, occasionally resting for a moment as the chill seeped into every part of Shay's body despite her layers of clothing and parka. They marched straight toward the parked plane but didn't see anyone in the cockpit. Shay left Lily resting inside. "It's okay, you saved my ass back there. I'm glad you're here." Shay brushed the gray hair out of Lily's face. "Rest and I'll be back before you know it."

Shay headed into the hangar connected to the only building present.

Once inside, she cautiously opened the door leading into a hallway. She savored the warmth for a minute before continuing. A male voice sounded from ahead, and she hurried toward it, reaching inside her parka to pull her gun if she ran into the witch.

The only people she saw were the pilot and another man she didn't recognize. They were sitting in a waiting room with two tables and chairs.

Shay lowered her hand. "Is Doctor Petrova here?"

The men exchanged glances, uncomfortable expressions on both their faces.

"It's important," the tomb raider barked.

"She...was here."

"Did she go back to the Repository?"

Shay could still catch her. The woman was powerful, but she'd be more limited inside a building compared to an ice and snowfield.

"No, she didn't. I don't even get it. Some unscheduled plane suddenly showed up. The pilot was a crazy son of a bitch. Petrova pulled up on a snowmobile and rushed onto the plane before the guy had even stopped, and..."

"And?"

"She lifted herself to the plane on ice. And had a wand. Pretty sure she was a witch."

Shay sighed and rubbed the bridge of her nose.

"Thanks." She snorted—might as well cover her tracks. "Pretty sure she stole something from the Repository."

"That would explain a lot."

The tomb raider slumped into a seat at the other table.

Even though she'd survived, she'd failed and would come back to the client empty-handed. Her reputation would take a hit, and even worse, a lot of things still didn't make sense.

A mercenary witch shouldn't have shown up in the middle of nowhere to snatch magic beans.

Shay still didn't know what the beans even did, or what the implications of Yulia having them were.

*Is that bitch a tomb raider, or is all this shit connected?*

## 11

The Ice Witch still haunted Shay's thoughts a couple days later. Peyton hadn't been able to track down any information, and the great Aletheia had had to admit to a client she wouldn't be able to deliver.

Lily's arm was a clean break and would heal nicely. She had a cast that Peyton quickly decorated in different colored pens and had set her up in his old space, even resurrecting some of the cubes. He had fussed with the pizza oven, trying to make Lily a pizza but so far the results were a lot of smoke and an oversized burned cracker.

Shay reassured Lily's worries about going out again by buying Lily her own tomb raiding belt, with a few accessories.

"You're just like Robin, now," said Peyton. "Your own utility belt."

As much as it bothered her, Shay didn't have time to fixate on the failed mission, or even Lily because the

Professor had contacted her for another quick job. Quick, but not necessarily safe, or so the man had told her.

She patted the bag of salt in her pocket. It wasn't all Morton's.

The salt had been mixed with the remnants of an enchanted stone allegedly used by a Renaissance-era wizard who had dabbled in spirit-summoning on the down low. It had kept him from the hangman's noose or worse.

*Don't worry, Miz Carson. Just sprinkle a little of this on them and the spirits will go running. Not saying there* will *be any, but better safe than sorry, right?*

"Your shit better work, Smite-Williams," Shay muttered to herself as she parked her rental truck in front of the decaying mansion.

Weeds and shrubs had long since completed their invasion of the yard, and holes marred the one proud Tudor-style mansion. What had once been a slice of elite living in upstate New York had since given way to complete ruin.

*Poor Halliday. No wonder you're haunting this place.*

Heiress Grace Halliday had an avid interest in the occult and had collected one of the more impressive collections of artifacts until her death in 1960. Her family had sold off everything, not believing that any of her so-called magical items had any real power. Even if most of them were garbage, the fact that Smite-Williams had sent the tomb raider proved that the woman had owned at least *some* magical artifacts.

Shay snickered, wondering if any of those people were still alive to regret their decision. Her target that afternoon was a small golden Celtic torc. The Professor had been cagey on the details, other than it had some dampening ability he'd need to make the best use of the jade from the Green Dragon Crescent Blade.

Between the vimana key and ancient weapon of legend, Shay wouldn't have been surprised if she woke up one day to find out that Smite-Williams had taken over the world.

*I guess it'll be a very drunken New World Order.*

The tomb raider stepped out of the vehicle, started toward the house, and froze. A translucent woman stared at her from the window and vanished a second later.

"Oh, fuck. So there's that. Guess that confirms why they could never sell this place."

Shay took a few deep breaths and headed toward the door. The torc hadn't been left behind. It'd been sold twice and mysteriously ended up back in the house twice, even if that wasn't a matter of public record.

After a few encounters with the spirits of the home, people—including a few wizards and witches—had decided to leave well enough alone. From what Shay had read, the confluence of magical energy in the area was unstable.

Previously, the haunting had involved only sounds or moving objects, but the flood of magic into Earth turned the haunted house into a genuine physical danger. If it hadn't been in the middle of nowhere, someone would probably have handled it already.

No one could agree if actual ghosts inhabited the house, or if they were the product of some artifact and the confluence of magical energies. Shay didn't really see that the details made much of a difference. She was going in, one way or another.

She kicked open the door. No ghost confronted her, just rotted wood and scurrying rats.

"The ghosts don't scare off the animals? Lazy assholes." She took a few careful steps inside. "Look, I don't want any trouble. Just need the torc, and I'll be out of your ghostly hair. Hell, if you want to steal it back from Smite-Williams, be my guest."

She assumed the Professor had some master plan to stop whatever curse or magic kept reclaiming the object. If not, maybe retrieving it would be a steady source of income.

The wind whispered in her ear, "Get...out."

Shay sucked in a breath and shook her head. "I can't do that. Maybe some other day I might consider it, but I'm coming off a recent loss, so it's kind of important that I complete this job." She walked toward the stairs. The last two reports had indicated that the torc always returned to the master bedroom.

A spectral form of a glaring man winked into existence at the bottom of the stairs.

"Come on, pal, you're already dead. Why the fuck do you even ca—"

A force smashed into Shay, knocking her clean across the room. She slammed into a wall with a grunt and fell to her knees.

"That fucking *hurt*, you dead asshole."

The ghost floated toward her. "Get...out."

Shay reached into her pocket. "Guess the recipe calls for a pinch of salt." She flung the enchanted salt at the ghost.

The form writhed and contorted its face, a howl of

unearthly pain echoing throughout the house. It blinked out of existence.

The tomb raider let out a sigh of relief. "Okay, so that shit works. Good to know. Too bad I have to give it back to the Professor."

Shay stood and dusted her hands on her pants.

"You...will...die...Shay...Carson."

"Oh, you know my name? Nice trick, assholes, but not worried about loser ghosts who can't even leave their house spreading the word."

She bounded up the steps, not wanting the ghosts to have any chance to throw her down the stairs. Two spectral forms, a man and a woman, guarded the hallway. She flung the salt at them and they vanished.

Dead or sent to the World in Between—who knew? Didn't matter. She was killing some ghosts. Maybe that was redundant.

The hallway contained six closed doors. Shay kicked in the first couple and found empty rooms. The third contained a scowling ghost of a woman in a dress that looked more *Little House on the Prairie* than 1960s. The tomb raider managed to toss some of her salt right before an invisible force smacked her into the hallway wall.

Shay took a deep breath and rubbed the back of her head. This was getting annoying.

The third room was also empty, and so were the next two.

Fortune mocked Shay, forcing her into the sixth room. At least she didn't have to look far. The torc sat in the middle of the room and shone brightly, as if it'd just been polished.

"There we go."

She snatched it up and spun on her heel. Three ghosts confronted her this time, frowning. Her free hand dropped to her pocket to grab some salt.

The tomb raider stopped just before throwing it. The ghosts should have thrown her around by now, but they were only glaring at her.

Shay lifted the torc and grinned. "Something about this is stopping you, huh?" She laughed and sauntered toward the spirits. They disappeared. "Yeah, thought so. Not so tough now, are you, you dead assholes?"

The tomb raider continued toward the stairs. A half-dozen spectral forms floated in the air, all wearing masks of hatred.

"Hey, don't hate me. I'm just doing a job." She gave a little wave. "Keep it fun. Keep it dead." She winked.

Shay snickered as she made her way to the car. A dozen translucent spirits now floated in front of the house, but that wasn't so bad. If she was going to piss somebody off, it might as well be somebody who was already dead.

*Yeah, fuck you, Yulia. You were just a blip in my badass career. Let's see you try your ice magic shit on* them.

---

Ghosts and Ice Witches made for annoying and exciting jobs, but Shay looked forward to visiting Alison at the new school and seeing how well she was adapting. She'd decided against telling Brownstone about any of her recent adventures or even her new tomb raider in training, just yet.

He didn't need to know about her failure, and the Catholic bounty hunter might take issue with her fucking with ghosts rather than bringing in a bunch of priests to do Last Rites.

She didn't feel any guilt. She was just doing a job. If the Church wanted to handle the house, that was on them.

It was Parents' Weekend at Alison's school, and she was going to enjoy it.

The girl waved happily from a table in the lunchroom as Shay and Brownstone maneuvered through the thick crowd of kids and parents.

"Look at this place," Brownstone exclaimed, gazing at all the elegant wooden tables and booths. "This looks more like a fancy restaurant than a school cafeteria."

When the pair got to the table, Alison got up and hugged them.

After they sat down Shay glanced around, taking in everything. The contrast between a magic school centered around teens and her experiences with deadly magic on her job stuck out in her mind. The implications of the place weren't lost on her either.

Just because a kid studied magic at the School of Necessary Magic didn't mean they'd grow up to be a good person, any more than all the asshole politicians who went to college at some fancy private school grew up to be good people. A future Snegurka might be already there.

The tomb raider shook her head, not wanting Alison to look into her soul and see any of her dark thoughts. As if raising a teenager with hormones wasn't tricky enough. Now they could see your soul or predict your future.

After they'd talked about Alison's classes and her

friends, Shay poked Brownstone with her elbow. "Don't put your baggage on her. And give Alison her present already."

After all, they'd both worked hard for it, including the recovery of the Green Dragon Crescent Blade. Once Brownstone explained what the Professor was offering him, Shay's respect for the man grew even more. He'd found a way to be overprotective and stylish at the same time.

Brownstone pulled out the jewelry box and opened it, revealing a jeweled pendant on a silver chain.

"The magic coming off of it! It's beautiful," Alison exclaimed.

"And functional."

"Huh?"

"It's called an 'Aegis Pendant.' It's a kind of shield. You activate it by wanting to be protected and saying 'Aegis aeon.' Once you do that, it'll form a magic shell right around your body."

"I love it," Alison replied. She hopped up and rushed over to pull him into a hug as tears ran down her cheeks.

Brownstone blinked. "Why are you crying if you like it?" Alison just looked at him and Shay rolled her eyes.

After a few moments, the girl hurried off to show her friends.

Shay shook her head. "You're a damn enigma, Brownstone."

"Huh?"

"Clueless one second, wise the next."

A s her own boss, Shay could take a vacation whenever she wanted. A week after visiting Alison at the school, she'd still avoided taking on any new jobs. It was even nice to take Lily out shopping for some new clothes and some decent pizza, leaving Peyton behind to play with the new oven.

Pounding out so many in a row might have done wonders for her reputation, even with the loss of the magic beans, but the tomb raiding world wouldn't fall under the control of Snegurka just because Shay didn't take on a job every other day.

Running herself ragged also increased the chance she'd make a mistake. She was still wondering if taking Lily with her was an asset or a mistake.

As annoying as the Antarctica situation had been, she hadn't screwed anything up. She'd just not gotten there in time. It didn't make the burn go away completely, but it dulled it.

The tomb raider sighed as she sat down at a table in

Warehouse Four with several piles of books in front of her. She wasn't sure about what irritated her more—that Yulia had snagged the beans before she had, or that the woman held her in such contempt that she hadn't finished her off.

*You're gonna regret letting me go, bitch.*

Shay shook her head. She wasn't going to worry about that for now. Today's little background research session was a follow-up to an already successful—if not particularly profitable—raid. She'd been practically living in Warehouse Four for the last few days, occasionally checking on Lily.

The stone she'd recovered from Mexico sat on the table next to her. Now that she'd had time to catch her breath, she had thrown herself into good old-fashioned research to figure out what the hell the thing was.

Something caused it to be worth the life of a tomb raider and special enough that some weird possessed elf didn't want to give it up.

Peyton was still looking into the stone, but she'd told him not to prioritize the work. He was more useful to her keeping an eye on the net and Lily was more than eager to help him. If Yulia surfaced Shay wanted to know right away, so she could roast the ice bitch.

Her internet searches into the stone and its symbols had proven useless so far, so she decided to just hit book after book in hopes that she might find something. A lot of accumulated knowledge still hadn't made it online, so she hadn't been worried that she'd not found anything in her initial checks.

What *did* trouble her was the lack of information now

that she'd dived into her rare book collection. She'd hoped for at least a hint of progress.

*Ancient Mesoamerican Language and Writing Systems: A New Unified Approach* and translated journals from missionaries all the way back to the Conquistadores hadn't turned up anything during the previous day's research session. She couldn't find anything that looked remotely like the symbols, not even if she squinted and tried to find vague similarities.

The day before that she'd hit some of her South Asia sources heavily, working on the theory that the stone might be related to a vimana. Hours and hours of skimming hadn't located anything familiar.

*A Modern Field Guide to Ancient Scripts* didn't help.

Her trip through *Oriceran Writing: An Academic Survey* proved no more useful than any of her other books.

Shay held up the stone and stared at the glyphs. The more she looked at the symbols, the stranger they seemed. Something about them was different from anything she'd ever encountered.

She thought back to what the elf had said about it.

*"It gives me hints. Places to visit. For the future."*

The words were English, but she had no idea what they meant.

His explanation could mean everything from the stone being a map to it being some sort of time-travel artifact, if such a thing even existed. She hadn't heard about time-travel magic, but it was hard to dismiss anything out of hand, no matter how outlandish.

*How would I know? Maybe some asshole keeps fucking with time, and we all don't notice because events reset?*

Shay chuckled. The thought didn't disturb her for some reason. No point in worrying about something she couldn't even begin to control.

She set down the stone and rubbed her chin.

One possibility was taking the stone to Tubal-Cain. She could ask him if he knew anything about it, but she was leery of presenting an unknown artifact to a gnome she had no reason to trust and who didn't seem to care whether she lived or died. Just because he'd made knives for her didn't mean he wouldn't seize a powerful artifact if given the chance.

No, she needed to keep the mystery in-house. Even the Professor didn't need to know. For all his smiles and friendship with Brownstone the man was still cryptic, and sometimes the only way to maintain control was to keep certain information private.

Secrets made the world go around, and everyone had more than a few.

Even though Peyton and Shay were tied together in a mutually beneficial relationship, he still didn't know she'd defused his dead man's switch, which meant she had the upper hand. He could keep his mouth shut, even if he *was* being a dumbass and using shadowy underworld companies to deliver pizza ovens.

That all meant, however, that he could be used as a resource once she had a better idea of where to direct the investigation. She also didn't want him to know just how desperate she was. Showing weakness or ignorance was never an advantage.

*I'll figure this shit out. This library isn't just for show.*

A few days later, Shay stifled a yawn as she opened another book and started flipping through the yellowed pages. True desperation had long since set in, and she'd stopped even trying to narrow her search by picking useful sources.

Instead, she'd settled on grabbing books and skimming through them until she found any diagrams or pictures she could compare to the symbols on the stone.

Small piles had grown into larger piles until she'd been forced to stop and re-shelve them all. If the situation continued, she'd have to look into if there was such a thing as an underworld library assistant.

*Damn, I have a lot of books. Maybe I should digitize all this shit someday. Then again, who would do the work? Purity?*

She snickered at the thought of creating a whole new underworld service industry.

Shay returned her attention to her current book. She hadn't even bothered to check the cover. At least it wasn't all that long. At this point, reading any of the text instead of focusing on the images was a waste of time.

She paged through a quarter, then half, then three-quarters of the book.

"Another whole lot of nothing. Yay."

She turned a page and froze, staring at the picture in the center of the new page. Her hands trembled in excitement.

The image depicted an iron obelisk unearthed on a Greek island. The writing didn't resemble anything from that area and most of it was unreadable, worn down by the elements, but she did recognize one of the symbols. She slid the stone next to the picture. Despite some minor stylistic differences, the similarity to one of the glyphs was unmistakable. She read the caption underneath the picture.

*This iron obelisk might be considered an out-of-place (OOP) artifact. The pillar was uncovered in a clearly bronze-age cultural stratum but is the product of advanced iron working. The unusual writing hasn't been linked to any extant or non-extant writing system, leading certain fringe theorists to suggest it might ultimately be of extraterrestrial origin, even though it's far more likely to be sourced from a lost regional language.*

"Aliens, huh?"

Shay flipped to the front of the book to check the copyright date, which was 1982. That was decades before the truth about Oriceran had come out.

She rubbed her chin. Everyone now assumed that all ancient alien reports involved Oricerans, but it was hard to be sure. So many things had changed. The writing didn't resemble anything from Oriceran that *she'd* been able to find, and the book's blithe assertion that it must be linked to another lost language didn't sit well. Very few non-Oriceran languages and writing systems couldn't be traced to something else in Earth's history.

*Places to visit.* Had he been talking about other planets?

Shay laughed, not sure if some ancient lost Oriceran language was a more outrageous theory than the idea that the writing had come from another planet harboring intelligent life.

It wouldn't hurt to follow up that angle.

*This shit is crazy. If aliens were real, people would have proof, just like we do with Oriceran, right?*

A few days later, Shay found herself sitting across from the Professor in the Leanan Sídhe. Even if she'd taken a little vacation, she wasn't going to say no when the man called her and offered her a job.

"It's a lovely evening, isn't it, Miz Carson?" The Professor was even rosier cheeked than usual. Father O'Banion might already be in control, which would be rare for a briefing.

"It's okay." Shay shrugged. "No one tried to kill me today. That's always a plus."

The older man shook his head. "What a sad, low bar both you and James set for your lives. I pity you at times."

"And what about you? What's a good day to Doctor F.J. Smite-Williams?"

"Any day I'm still breathing." He sipped some beer. "I should have been dead years ago. I've lived ten men's lives, and the fact that I continue to exist is a miracle in of itself." He held up the glass. "It's the alcohol. It's like ambrosia to the ancient Olympian gods."

"Maybe, but you're a careful guy."

He winked. "Well, it doesn't hurt to create your own miracles."

Shay chuckled. "Your text said you had a job for me. I liked the amount of money you mentioned, so I'm here."

He took a gulp of his drink and set it down. "Aye, Miz Carson. Are you familiar with the Ainu?"

"They were the native inhabitants of northern Japan. Same story as elsewhere—the new guys showed up, took control, and tried to erase the culture. Same song, different verse, et cetera. Not many of them left."

"True. The artifact I'm interested in is an Ainu sacred carving of a bear. It has come to my attention that it may be at an abandoned Shinto shrine in Hokkaido."

Shay frowned. "Wait, I thought Shinto wasn't an Ainu thing?"

"Traditionally, no, but it's flexibly syncretic belief system. Besides, I don't know the complete history of the artifact, only that it may be at this shrine. I want it, and as I mentioned in the message, I'm willing to pay handsomely for it."

"What's it do?"

The Professor smiled. "It's a type of magic modulator."

"Modulator?"

"It allows otherwise incompatible types of magic to be mixed. More importantly, it's incredibly dangerous in its present state, and I'll be loaning you a special pouch to contain it. Once you locate it, get it into the pouch as soon as possible."

"Or what?"

Smite-Williams lifted his hands, made fists, then stretched out all his fingers at once. "*Boom*. At least if you try to transport it without the pouch for too long a distance. If that energy is released, unusual magic can happen."

Shay nodded. "Duly noted. Now, who else is coming for it, and do they have magic anti-nuke bags?"

"That's the question now, isn't it? At least one other group of less-than-reputable tomb raiders is interested, but I'm more concerned about something else."

Shay frowned. "Other than the fact it might blow up?"

"Aye. I've been trying to track this artifact for some time. Without giving too much away, let's just say that I'm surprised to see it pop up, as it were, so recently."

"What do you think that means?"

"I don't know. That's why I'm hiring you to go and find it."

Shay stared at the Professor for a moment. "I'm surprised you don't want me to bring Brownstone."

He shrugged. "Some jobs require a hammer, others require a scalpel. I have the utmost confidence that you'll be able to handle this without additional aid. This is a situation where I'd prefer less violence."

"No guarantees."

The Professor smiled. "Just saying that James has a way of escalating situations."

"True enough." Shay nodded. "Okay, then, Professor, I'll go find you a bear carving."

S hay's car rumbled along the dirt road. According to
the GPS, it would still be about thirty more minutes
before she arrived at the temple. She couldn't complain too
much, considering the job didn't involve her having to go
to the middle of Antarctica or swim into a maze of
unstable logs.

Her phone rang and she glanced down at the caller ID.
Peyton.

"What's up?" she answered.

"I can barely hear you," he responded, static crowding
the line.

"You're not so great yourself. Huh, surprised I'm having
trouble. I mean, I'm a little off the beaten path, but not that
far. I'd have expected a better signal in the satellite mode.
Anyway, what's up, Peyton? Lily okay?"

*I'm actually worrying about her. Maybe I should send the kid
to the same school as Alison. Would she even go?*

"Lily's fine. She doesn't want me to tell you that she's
been working out. Ow!"

"I don't think you're supposed to rat somebody out while they're standing next to you."

"That's the only righteous way to do it. Ow! Hit me again, you one-armed bandit and I'll hit you back. I mean it!"

Shay rolled her eyes. "I'm hanging up now."

"No wait, don't! I had a reason for calling. A very good one. I figured I should pass something along to you. I was poking around on some dark web forums, and, I, uh…I spotted something nasty."

Shay laughed. "Hey, everybody has their own fetishes. We shouldn't judge." She stopped the car. It was hard enough to hear her assistant over the crap connection without the rumble of the road noise.

Peyton groaned. "Not nasty as in porn."

"What then?"

"Somebody's making a big move on Brownstone."

"Define big."

"A half-million general bounty available to *anyone* who kills him. Some sites are mentioning that a million might even be on the table."

Shay whistled. "Shit, really?"

"Uh-huh. They want him dead in a big way."

Shay sucked in a breath and slowly let it out. "That's a lot of money. It's gonna bring every wannabe out of the shadows, let alone the pros. Fuck, *I'd* take a whack at him for that much if I was still in the biz."

"What are we going to do about it?"

"I'm in the middle of a raid so I can't break and run for Brownstone, but the least I can do is let him know what's coming."

"Maybe I should."

"No," Shay responded. "For now, Brownstone doesn't need to know all of my business or yours."

"You mean, don't tell him about the t-e-e-n-a-g-e-r."

"I can spell you idiot."

Shay could hear Lily through the phone.

"Well, you never know if there's school in underground sewer tunnels."

"Nuclear escape tunnel, asshole."

"Shay, I can tell him without mentioning certain details."

"I'll handle it…and Peyton? Good job."

"No problem. Talk to you later." He disconnected.

Shay sighed. She'd give the bounty hunter a call and then get back to work. He was a big boy who could take care of himself. The man had already killed hundreds of Harriken, after all.

A true killer thought and acted differently. They were way more dangerous. She should know. She used to be one.

She dialed the bounty hunter to deliver the bad news.

---

*Stupid, Brownstone being so cocky. I don't think he gets that a load of hurt's coming for him. He should be a little more worried.*

The male ego was an impressive thing, both fragile and powerful at the same time. Brownstone seemed to relish the idea someone would be sending hitmen after him.

Shay had thought she'd all but talked herself out of

giving a damn, but now she was forced to admit a little concern had crept in.

It wasn't her problem. She was halfway across the world, and the Professor needed her to be Shay the Tomb Raider, not Shay the Brownstone Babysitter.

She tried to keep reminding herself that the bounty hunter might not have any reason to worry. The man could take a direct shotgun blast with the help of his magical amulet. That meant the average hitman going after him didn't have a chance.

The issue was the not-so-average hitmen. Witches, wizards, and other creatures might be able to pierce his defenses.

Shay shook her head. She needed to concentrate on the job at hand. Once she finished in Japan, she might consider offering Brownstone help if he wanted it. Maybe.

She frowned at something up ahead and pulled her car to the side of the dirt road.

*Fucking perfect. Just what my day needed.*

Two black SUVs with tinted windows were parked farther up. Someone had already beat her to the site. A look to her side had her groaning for a different reason.

She liked a good workout, but not in the middle of a job. A massive series of stone steps led up a steep hill to the temple site, flanked by dense trees on both sides. She'd seen the stairs in the satellite image but seeing them in person drove home just how many she would have to climb to get to the summit.

*Huh. Gotta respect all the guys who carried up the shit they needed to build the place.*

She didn't spot the *torii*, the traditional crossbeam Shinto gate, at the top of the stairs.

That surprised her, because she'd examined satellite photos of the area. Although much of the temple structure had caved in, the gate had still been standing in satellite images taken only a few days prior. Maybe the SUV boys'd had something to do with that.

The tomb raider wasn't about to hike all the way up the stairs to be ambushed.

It was time for a little drone survey. If the other tomb raiders spotted it and shot it down, at least she'd know where they were.

Before deploying the drone, she headed over to the SUVs and peered inside each. The tinting was light enough that she could tell both were empty.

Shay headed back to her car and pulled out the drone. She placed the machine on the ground, then activated her control app on her phone along with the surveillance feed.

The drone whirred and rose into the sky. She kept it close to the tree line as it followed the path of the hill and stairs. Even if the other tomb raiders spotted the machine, it was better than her stumbling into them and taking some bullets.

She saw debris on the stairs as the drone rose. Pieces of scorched wood. Rocks. Some metal.

"What the fuck?"

Shay stared at the feed, not sure what she was seeing at first when the drone reached the top of the hill. There should have been the remains of an old Shinto temple, but instead, there was only a large crater.

She increased the drone's altitude. The scorched

remains of the base of the *torii* still stood at the top of the stairs. The wood on the stairs appeared to be pieces that had been blown from the structure.

The massive crater spread across most of the clearing that had once marked the temple area. Trees around the area had been knocked over and were also scorched as if some massive bomb had blasted the area.

Shay sighed and fished out her phone. Under most circumstances she'd never think about contacting a client in the middle of the raid, but this wasn't most situations and Smite-Williams wasn't most clients.

"Tell me the good news," the Professor answered, his voice slurred. It was hard to understand him over the weak connection.

"The other guys got here first, and it's obvious that they didn't bring a special bag."

"Oh...I see. One moment." The slur in his voice vanished.

Shay continued to stare at the drone feed, marveling at the thoroughness of the destruction. Not a single scrap of the temple remained.

The Professor cleared his throat on the other end. "My information suggests you can still find it."

"I'm telling you it's gone. This place is a crater."

"No, it's just released some...energy." The Professor chuckled. "Unfortunately, my information also suggests it's likely no longer in Japan, but I can't tell you where it is now."

"You can't, or you won't?"

"I can't. I want the item in question, so if I had more information I'd give it to you. The fact that it's already had a little incident will make it harder to track for some time, but fortunately, it also makes it less dangerous and useless for some time. This may be something we have to put on a backburner for a while unless you can find some other clues."

"Uh, that's less than helpful."

"Aye, but you're a professional, so I'll leave it to you. I don't hold this against you. I'll pay you the rest of your fee when you recover it, and I understand it might take a few more weeks. Right now I have a few dirty limericks to dispense."

"Priorities."

"Exactly, Miz Carson."

He hung up.

So much for a low-key job. Now there was a crater and she needed to find more leads, but at least the Professor was taking it well.

She sighed and navigated the drone back down to her vehicle. It was time to get a little cardio and view the damage directly.

Minutes later the tomb raider crested the hill. The crater was even more magnificent to the naked eye and extended deep into the ground.

Shay retrieved her AR goggles from her backpack and examined the area using several different frequencies, but didn't find anything unusual. She'd been half-expecting some residual thermal energy in the crater, but it matched the background temperature.

"The artifact is still around? How can he be sure? Nothing could have survived this."

After a few more minutes of inspecting the crater, Shay

made her way back down to the black SUVs. Both were locked.

Shay grabbed a universal key remote from a box in the back of her car. She didn't have much use for the gadget under normal circumstances, but since her adventure with a damaged car in Russia she'd started to bring it along on raids in case she needed to *borrow* someone's vehicle to escape. Soon both vehicles were unlocked.

Shay slipped on some gloves. No reason to leave any fingerprints for the Japanese police.

The vehicles were clean, with stickers indicating they were rentals from a place in Sapporo. There was nothing in the back of either: no weapons, no drones, no equipment.

Shay looked back up the stairs. The poor bastards were dust now. *Or were they?* The Professor seemed convinced the artifact was still around, but if it'd blown up the other tomb raiders it shouldn't have been able to go anywhere else.

*Unless those fuckers* meant *to set it off, for some reason.*

The sedans didn't have any dust, leaves, or any other indications they'd been there for any length of time.

Shay checked for nearby cities on her map app. There was a small town about an hour away. It wouldn't hurt to check.

The tomb raider popped the back hatch of the first SUV and pulled up the back mat covering the spare tire. The tire was absent, and several guns and gadgets lay inside.

She chuckled.

*This seems like some shit Brownstone would pull.*

Shay preferred her equipment to always be available.

A cell phone lay next to one of the guns and she took it. At least she had a lead if she couldn't find out anything in town.

She touched the screen, then frowned at the lock screen.

Shay pulled out her phone and dialed Peyton.

"I don't have anything new about Brownstone," he answered.

"If I brought you a cell phone could you break into it?"

"Sure. No big deal."

She could almost hear the grin in his voice.

"Okay, then I'm bringing home a present. Talk to you later." She hung up.

Maybe she didn't have the item, but if the other tomb raiders had it the phone would lead her right to them. Even if they'd been vaporized, their friends might have some clues she didn't.

───────

"Big blue explosion," the bar owner offered, gesturing with his hands. He rattled off something in Japanese to one of the other customers, and she nodded her head in agreement.

Shay brought up her phone and tapped the translate function. She didn't need quality for this conversation. "Please repeat that," she said into the phone.

The phone rattled off her request in Japanese.

The man repeated himself.

"Foreigners came in black cars," her phone translated.

"Then drove up to the old temple. Then a big explosion. We could see it all the way from here."

"Thanks."

Shay had asked a half-dozen people if they'd seen anything, but everyone gave her the same basic story. Some non-Japanese men drove up, the temple exploded in a bright blue flash, and no one came back. According to the news, a plane had crashed in the area.

She snorted at the thought. She'd been there a little over an hour before and hadn't seen any crashed plane. The Japanese government obviously knew a magical explosion had occurred and were covering up the truth. It was funny how even after the truth of Oriceran had come out, so many people still lied about magic.

The job was on hold until she could get the phone to Peyton.

Shay blew out a breath. It wouldn't hurt to follow up at the rental place in Sapporo and check out the site again. If she couldn't find anything, she could head back home to help Brownstone out in his war against… Well, probably everybody.

The tomb raider laughed.

*Yeah, that is the smart play. Damn, Brownstone, if you weren't such a badass I wouldn't even want to help you. Funny how that works.*

# 1 4

S hay grumbled as she sat on the edge of the soft hotel bed. There was nothing like traveling halfway around the world only to find your target site was now a huge crater. At least she hadn't been in the place when it'd become a hole.

Now that the field archaeologist was back in civilization she needed to catch up on her mail and messages, so she pulled out her phone and started skimming the subject lines of her messages. One in particular caught her eye, and she opened it to read the detail.

"Oh, shit," Shay muttered. "Damn. Guess that explains it." She immediately dialed Brownstone.

After their brief and unsatisfactory conversation, Shay gritted her teeth and slammed her phone down on the nightstand so hard her fingers hurt. She shook them out and looked at her screen, which now sported a jagged crack

"This might have been a cheap burner phone, Brownstone, but I'm still gonna make you pay for it," Shay ranted.

"All this stupid machismo crap from men and their stubborn asses. Plus... You know what, Brownstone? I'm gonna make you pay for the airline ticket too.

"Damn the man! He needs to get his head in the game and take this threat seriously. And what the hell was up with asking me to take care of Alison? "

---

Shay leaned back in her seat, enjoying the comfort and space that came with first class. A first-class ticket on a supersonic flight wasn't cheap, but Brownstone would be paying for it eventually, one way or another.

"Ladies and gentlemen," came a voice over the speaker. "This is Captain Smith. I regret to inform you that we'll have to take a detour to Seattle. Storm activity over the Pacific is unusually severe, and we've received word there may be some sort of magical fluctuations. We'll land in Seattle and wait a few hours, then continue on to Los Angeles. We're sorry for any inconvenience this may cause."

She was racing back to Los Angeles to help Brownstone. Any delay meant the chance of him doing something stupid or dying increased.

"Brownstone," she muttered. "Even trying to come home and save you has to be a pain in the ass."

---

*One more delay and I'm gonna fucking lose it.*

The whole point of hopping on a supersonic flight was

to get her back to Los Angeles as soon as possible, not get routed to Seattle and wait around for another flight. Now that she was finally on a flight back to her original destination, she still couldn't relax.

Shay had given the Professor a quick call to inform him she'd be following up on the raid after Brownstone's issues were settled. He didn't seem to mind or care. With the artifact having already exploded, the man's urgency concerning the Ainu carving had vanished.

Even if *he* didn't care, the tomb raider cared. She didn't have time to run off trying to save Brownstone's ass every time he got in trouble—which had been a lot lately.

*Fucking Brownstone. This is shitty timing.*

But it wasn't his fault. It was the damned Harriken.

Shay frowned. The Harriken were idiots. The assholes should have learned their lesson and left the man alone. If the hitmen didn't take him down, he was only going to come at them again.

And she'd help him.

The tomb raider blinked at the realization. It wasn't attraction motivating her, even if she didn't mind a peek or two at Brownstone's muscles. It was something deeper. Respect.

She didn't understand a lot of what went on in the bounty hunter's mind, but between his skills and the way he'd thrown himself into looking after Alison, her esteem kept rising.

Even with half the underworld of LA bearing down on him, Brownstone seemed more concerned with Alison than his own life. It also meant he accepted he might die.

*You're just a man in the end, huh? I can respect that. That fear might just keep you alive. The cocky ones always die in the end.*

It shouldn't have been any of her business if killers came after Brownstone, but she'd made it hers when she helped him assault the Belmont House. She'd had her chance to stay out of it, but had run right into the thick of the killings.

*What the fuck ever. Might as well help finish what I started, and I don't like these cocky Harriken bastards.*

Someone yelled a few seats behind her. That was what she got for not shelling out for first-class between Seattle and Los Angeles. Shay might be a foul-mouthed ex-killer, but that didn't mean she wasn't a travel snob. She'd thought the quick trip from Seattle to Los Angeles wouldn't necessitate the upgrade.

"Don't you get it?" the voice yelled. "It's all a trick. Lemons? Limes? They're the same damn thing, and I'm tired of everyone pretending otherwise. Wake up, sheeple."

Shay frowned and looked over her shoulder. A red-faced man gesticulated wildly from his seat at a worried-looking flight attendant. Someone took their citrus very damned seriously.

The flight attendant put a hand in front of her. "There's no reason to yell. You need to calm down, sir. I think you've just had a little too much to drink."

Perfect. First the damned storm, and now some drunk asshole freaking out. If the man got out of control, the pilot would land the plane early and she'd end up delayed again in some annoying place like Sacramento.

*You better calm down if you don't want me involved, asshole.*

The man shoved the flight attendant, and she yelped and fell. The woman scrambled back to her feet.

The drunk shot out of his seat. "Don't tell me to fucking calm down. I will *not* fucking calm down! Not while all this bullshit is going on!"

The flight attendant ran toward the front of the plane, her eyes wide.

Shay unbuckled her seatbelt and stood. The universe hated her. Maybe not as much as Brownstone, but still.

"Hey, asshole. That woman asked nicely. *I'm* telling you rudely. Sit your ass back in that chair and shut your yap, or I will sit you there, and you won't like how I do it."

The man rounded on her, his eyes wild. "You don't tell me what to do. I can talk about fruit all I want. It's my damned right as an American. What did we even have the Revolution for?"

"Not to debate lemons and limes." Shay shrugged. "Look, I don't give a shit what you want to talk about, but you need to sit your ass down so they don't land this plane before we arrive in Los Angeles. I have an important appointment."

The man squared his shoulders. "Fuck you, bitch."

The tomb raider glared at him and moved forward. "Okay, now we're gonna count down to one. Three..."

"I have the right to express my opinions on lemons and limes! This is America, not Denmark."

*Denmark? Huh? Wait, I can't get caught up in his bullshit. I need to end this.*

"Two..."

The man shook his fist at her. "Who the fuck are you

supposed to be, an air marshal? I'll take this whole plane down if I need to."

"One." Shay rolled her eyes and laid him out with one punch. He fell to the ground, groaning.

She shook out her fist and hurried back to her seat to grab her backpack. A few seconds later, she returned to the man with a roll of duct tape in hand.

The other passengers watched her with a mixture of confusion and curiosity.

"Don't worry. I'm a pro." Shay pushed the half-stunned man into his seat. The rip of duct tape filled the cabin as she treated the man as if he were a leaky pipe, starting with his mouth.

The co-pilot and two flight attendants ran down the aisle and stopped a few feet behind Shay, astonishment on their faces.

Shay continued taping the man into his seat. "Always be prepared. Duct tape is a necessity on all trips."

The other passengers cheered and applauded.

The flight attendant from before approached Shay. "Are you an air marshal? I didn't realize we had one on the flight."

Shay shook her head. "A teacher."

"Oh, I get it. You've done this before."

"Something like that."

"Thank you. Is there anything we can do to pay you back? We can at least offer you complimentary drinks."

Shay shook her head. "If you really want to show your gratitude, make sure this plane lands in Los Angeles." She pointed with her thumb at the duct-taped man. "He's not going anywhere."

*Finally!*

Shay yanked her phone out of her pocket and turned it on as she hurried down the LAX jetway. She winced as she spotted the missed call from Brownstone.

She played the message he'd left as she stepped into the boarding gate.

"Hey, Shay, it's me. You know me…I hate to ask anyone for a favor, but I'm trying to be real about how shit might end up in the next few days." He took a deep breath. "Look, don't know if you're coming back, but if you are, don't come to LA. I'd rather you stayed with Alison until I figure out how to take care of the Harriken and get this hit taken care of. The Harriken know about her, even if they don't know where she is. For all I know, they might still think they can weasel her mother's inheritance out of her.

"Yeah, I know what you're thinking. She's in a magic school surrounded by a bunch of wizards and witches who could turn their asses into toads or whatever. I thought she'd be safe there, but now I'm not sure. Maybe it's like in *Raiders of the Lost Ark* where the guy has the sword and Indy just pulls out the gun. You know, like don't bring a magic wand to a gunfight. How many of these magical asshole professors have ever been in a fight? How do I know they don't have some stupid rules about killing bastards who come for them?"

"Anyway, I'd appreciate it if you make sure Alison is okay. And thank you. You make a hell of an aunt."

Shay let out a sigh, her left hand cradling her forehead.

A few more steps moved Shay away from the stream of

disembarking people, and she rubbed the back of her neck as she thought about her next course of action.

*Damn it, Brownstone. Why did you have to make this harder than it already was?*

The field archaeologist hurried toward baggage claim, still trying to decide what the hell she should even do.

Brownstone could be right about the school.

Of course, a hitman who could use magic was a different matter entirely.

Shay stepped on an escalator. Even if the hitman didn't have the same power level or skills as the teachers at the school, he still might be able to take them out.

The problem with violence was that people misunderstood what made a dangerous killer versus a victim.

The key wasn't what tool a person used.

If Brownstone had made that call he was in over his head, which meant he needed her help. But he'd also asked her to watch Alison.

A long groan escaped Shay's lips.

---

Peyton would never be able to kick ass like Shay or Brownstone or even Lily, but there was one skill he could learn that would impress the hardened ex-killer.

He patted his long, white apron and smiled at the stone oven in the corner. It had taken a little work to get proper venting set up, but now it was ready and aching for him to use it and deliver some good old-fashioned pizza to his stomach.

*Maybe I'll open my own pizza place. Cooking has to be easier than what I do on a computer every day. It's just about following a recipe. How hard could that be?*

Peyton cracked his knuckles and moved over to the small folding table he'd set up to hold his ingredients.

"You ready for this?" He grinned at Lily who even managed a smile. He had drawn a decent rendition of a flying dragon over the multi-colors on her cast. Having her around was even making him miss his beastly family less.

"It's not too late to order something. Purity Solutions could even pick it up. I'm starving." Lily patted her belly.

"You're always starving. It's your resting state. Have a little faith. I can figure this out."

Yeast, flour, salt, and a little water. It was almost the simplest recipe in the world. It wasn't like he was making mole sauce.

"One teaspoon? Hmm." He measured out some yeast and added it to a bowl on the table. "Huh. Wait. That was one tablespoon, but it shouldn't make that much of a difference. Way more flour than yeast anyway. I'm sure it's just an order of magnitude thing."

Peyton added the water, flour, and salt and then started whisking away while humming.

"This is kind of relaxing, actually. Wait, added too much flour. Probably should add some more yeast to balance it out. A couple more tablespoons shouldn't hurt. Still a lot more flour." He nodded.

"Are you talking to me or the pizza."

"Then it's time to knead. Watch out, Shay, I'm going to make all other pizzas seem like garbage."

"The pizza." Lily sat back on a chair and opened a magazine.

Peyton grimaced as the overpowering yeast stench from the oven assaulted his nostrils. The smell mixed with the pepperoni scent. Bile rose in his throat.

Lily covered her mouth as she waved the magazine in the air. "What the hell did you do? It smells like a sewer backed up in here. Is that what happened?"

The warehouse didn't have a lot in the way of natural airflow, so no matter where he walked, a smothering cloud of yeast nastiness waited to choke him and remind him of his awful failure.

"This is...not good. *So* not good." He shook his head. "Okay, so there *is* such a thing as too much yeast. Good to know." He picked up the pizza and tossed it into a trash can. "I've got to air this place out before someone calls a HAZMAT team."

"If you leave the loading bay doors open Shay will point her gun at your head. Does the ceiling open up? What? There's a lot of weird shit in these warehouses. An opening ceiling would not be even in the top ten."

Peyton shook his head. "No opening up there, although not a bad idea for my to-do list. I can figure out how to deal with the smell later. I still need to get a halfway decent pizza finished, and now I know to use the measurements in the recipe and not be so inexact."

"You're talking to the pizza again, aren't you. Fuck, dude, I'm going out for some air. You stay in this if you want to and I'm taking cash from the petty cash drawer."

"That was my secret stash."

"Found it the first night and I was on pain killers. You

would die in the wild." Lily tucked two twenties in her pocket and headed for the side door.

"I've been in the field before," Peyton protested.

"How'd that go? I thought so," said Lily, as she pulled the door behind her.

Peyton grimaced as he tilted his head and calculated how much yeast he'd added.

*Okay, maybe nine times as much as called for was a little excessive.*

With a renewed respect for quantities Peyton prepared new dough, humming as he kneaded and rolled it out.

"It's not just about the oven," he murmured. "And if I can't mess with the recipe much, it's got to be about technique. That's got to be the key. Might as well do it like the pros."

Peyton picked up the dough and tossed it in the air. It couldn't be that difficult. After all, he'd seen it done countless times at the pizza places Shay had taken him to.

"This isn't so..." he stared down at his now dough-covered shoe, "hard."

---

Peyton's stomach rumbled as he stuck the wooden pizza paddle underneath his latest attempt at an edible pizza and transferred it to a tray. His prep had included perfect measurements and no clever dough-handling stunts. Everything was finally going according to plan.

Sure, the whole building still smelled like he'd fallen into a yeast vat, but he'd gotten used to it.

All the suffering and trials had led to this point. He'd

taste the delicious pepperoni pizza he'd made with his own two hands and remember that no man improved himself without some setbacks.

"I wonder if Shay would get mad if I started calling myself 'the Pizza King?'" Peyton chuckled and shook his head.

He paced in front of the pizza, giving it a few more minutes to cool.

The steel of the pizza cutter glinted in the light as he lifted it.

"I declare thee the first victim of the Pizza King. Your crime? Being too delicious."

Peyton sliced the pizza into six pieces and picked up one. The color looked decent. Maybe a little more cheese was in order and the pepperoni could have been sliced with more consistency, but it wasn't half-bad.

The delicious smell made his stomach gurgle again, and he bit down.

Peyton managed to keep the bite in his mouth a whole three seconds before he spat it out. So much for taste aligning with smell.

"What the hell? I followed the damn recipe, so why does it taste like vinegar and soy sauce had a baby together on my pizza?" Peyton dropped his face into his hands. "The rebels are winning. The Pizza King may be deposed. Where's Lily with some food?"

---

Peyton sighed as he finished putting his ingredients away in the breakroom cabinet and refrigerator. Lily had taken pity on him and brought back a burger and fries, still warm.

"I still don't understand what I did wrong."

"The way I see it, it's like my training. More complicated than it looks on the surface but if you're willing to hang in there, you'll get it. Of course, tell Shay about my business like working out already, again and I'll bust apart your oven."

"Deal. We should stick together. I only pray that Shay doesn't decide to watch the warehouse surveillance feed. She might never reveal her secret warehouse to me after witnessing the catastrophe."

"What do you think is in there?"

"Could be anything. Men held in suspended animation. Magical artifacts all her own. I don't know, I'm out. That's all I have."

"You're bent, dude," said Lily, slurping up the rest of her chocolate milkshake.

"Did you bring me one of those? That hurts."

"One good arm. Be glad for what you did get."

Peyton's phone rang, and he pulled it out of his pocket. Shay. It was like she knew what he'd done. Maybe she had watched the feed. He waved frantically at Lily to be quiet.

"What? She knows I live here."

"Hey, Shay."

"Just wanted you to know there's been a change in plans," Shay explained.

"What?"

"I'm going to Virginia to stay with Alison until Brownstone gets his shit cleaned up."

"Seriously?"

"Yeah. I've already contacted the Professor about the job."

"Need me or Lily to do anything?" Peyton asked.

"Nope. When I come back you'll need to check out the phone, but nothing before then. Don't do anything stupid or make a mess and you'll be fine."

Peyton glanced at the closed refrigerator.

*I cleaned up the mess. The Pizza King is not yet vanquished.*

Shay cleared her throat. "Just thought of something."

Peyton winced. *Please don't ask about the pizza.*

"Since the Ainu thing's on the backburner, go ahead and look into those symbols. I've got some interesting leads, but I want to see what you turn up."

"Oh, sure. Will do."

"Don't call me unless it's important." Shay hung up.

He let out a sigh of relief. He'd say one thing for online magical research—it didn't end with the building smelling awful.

"You look like you got away with something, Peyton. Keep a perspective. It's smelly pizza. Not like you gave away our location or something."

---

A lison smiled. "I'm glad you're going to be able to spend the next few days with me, and I'm sorry I can't cancel all my stuff."

Shay shrugged. "Don't worry about it. I was just in the area and figured I'd stop by. You never know when I'll be able to, so I might as well when I can, right?"

"I'll be back in my room in an hour." Alison waved as she stepped out of the lunchroom.

Shay forced a smile on her face as she sat back down at a table. The school agreed to let her stay for a few days. She found herself wanting to call and check on Lily even more. Something about seeing all these teenagers running around worrying about passing a test in Spells class.

Shay hadn't bothered to lie to the headmistress, even though she'd not given Alison any hint of the truth about why she was there. Something about Headmistress Berens told her it'd be pointless.

*Fucking witch or elf—whatever the hell she is.*

Instead, Shay had explained how Alison's foster father

had gotten wrapped up in some trouble with unsavory characters. Not that it was hard to figure it out given some of the news coverage coming out of LA

The staff didn't seem worried. They all but laughed the threat off.

"I think you'll find," the headmistress had explained, "that this school has excellent defenses."

There was only one problem with Shay's brilliant plan. Alison had material to study and friends to chat with, and the headmistress didn't want Shay following the girl all over campus or disturbing the students.

That had led to her eating chicken soup in the cafeteria and thumbing through her phone in the middle of the afternoon to check dark web forums for updates on Brownstone.

A young dark-haired elf girl around Alison's age wandered by the table with a tray in hand.

Shay narrowed her eyes. Something about the girl seemed very familiar. Tension suffused into her muscles. She didn't want to freak out on some poor kid Brownstone-style, but it wasn't like she'd dealt with a lot of elves, let alone elf kids. She couldn't just ignore this instinct.

*Is this some sort of Yulia shit?*

The elf girl stopped and blinked at Shay. "Something wrong?"

Shay shook her head. "Sorry, just looking around."

The girl nodded. "Hey, you're Alison's sort-of aunt, right?"

"Yeah, you could say that." The tomb raider laughed. "Shay."

The girl set her tray on the table and sat across from Shay. "Izzie."

"Izzie, huh? Didn't expect that."

"What?"

Shay shrugged. "I don't know. I guess I still have this stereotype that elves will have names like Windsong or something."

"Maybe some Wood Elves. I don't know." The girl chuckled. Her smile vanished. "It was good of you and Mr. Brownstone to bring Alison here."

"Oh? Glad you approve."

Izzie nodded. "It must have been tough to lose her parents like that, but it's really cool how you and Mr. Brownstone are helping her."

"It's more him than me."

Shay couldn't help but stare at the girl. The sense of familiarity had only grown with the conversation, both with her appearance and her voice. It went beyond the sensation of having spotted her during an earlier visit to the school. Shay had barely talked to any of the students in her previous visits, let alone this girl.

"What about you, Izzie?" Shay inquired. "Come from fifty generations of grand elf masters of magic or something?"

The girl sighed and shrugged. "Maybe."

"Maybe?"

"I grew up in an orphanage. I never knew my parents."

"Kind of like a guy I know."

Izzie blinked. "Huh?"

Shay waved a hand. "Don't worry about it, kid. Tough break." She nodded toward the door. "But now you're in a magic school, so not everything's bad. But you better eat your food before it gets cold."

"Oh right. Yeah. Thanks." Izzie smiled and picked up her fork.

Shay forced a smile as she watched the girl. Instinct had saved her life many times, and she didn't want to ignore it now. Her instincts screamed that the orphanage story was bullshit.

The simplest explanation was that the girl was lying. She might be an elf at a magic school, but she was still a teen. She might crave a special background to impress people with. She might also be confused.

Magic sat at the heart of a much darker explanation: the spell on the front gate affected people's memories. It wasn't so hard to imagine the girl was under some sort of enchantment.

"Great school you've got here," Shay offered.

Izzie nodded and smiled.

"Do the teachers keep a close eye on the students?"

"For the most part."

"Glad to hear it."

*It's a good thing I'm spending a few days here to keep an eye on Alison, just in case the threat's inside the gate already.*

---

Alison was sleeping...finally. Shay was still wired from her day.

Alison's phone rang and Shay rushed to grab it. She hurried into the bathroom, closed the door, and answered the call.

"Alison, I hope it's not too late," Brownstone's deep voice began. "I figured I'd call as soon as I got a chance, and it's just...been a busy day."

"It's me," Shay told him. "Alison's asleep."

They filled each other in on what was happening, which, given it involved Harriken bounties and exploding artifacts, took a while.

The rustle of Alison shifting in bed caught Shay's attention.

"Okay, I think I better go. Stay alive."

"I'm trying. Talk to you later." Brownstone hung up.

Shay glanced down at Alison.

*So this is what it means to care. It doesn't hurt as much as I thought it would.*

---

Shay sat on the edge of the bed while Alison showered.

The teen emerged from the bathroom in a robe, her hair still wet.

"Look, Alison," Shay said. "I think I should be a little more honest about what's going on with Brownstone. I kind of gave you a line about what was going on, but that's not really the whole truth. I thought about lying to protect you, but I think—"

"You shouldn't lie to me," Alison told her, tilting her head.

Shay held up a hand. "Yeah, yeah, I know. Lying's bad and all that. Like I said, I *thought* about it, but I decided against it. After everything you've gone through, you deserve to know when bad things are happening so you can figure out how you want to deal with them your own way."

The girl shook her head. "No, you don't understand, Aunt Shay. I can tell when people are lying to me now. Most of the time, anyway."

Shay blinked. "You can tell when people are lying? That's...handy. That's *very* handy."

As Shay explained Brownstone's situation, the teen's lips pursed and a dark expression settled over her face.

"Are you okay?" Shay asked when she'd finished.

Alison nodded. "I'm just...tired of people hurting the people I love. I'll admit that I don't like feeling this way, but I'm experiencing an overwhelming urge to hurt people."

Shay sat down next to Alison and pulled her into an embrace. "Don't worry, Alison. We're gonna make sure you never have to."

Shay sipped her margarita. The Charlottesville bar she'd selected was a nice low-key place. Light country played in the background, but the crowd seemed more upscale than cowboy.

The ambiance was secondary. A little booze after the last few days was hitting the spot.

She hadn't minded spending the peaceful days with Alison, but regret still lingered in her heart. She let out a little chuckle, thinking about how the bounty hunter had solved his problem in the most ridiculous and over-the-top Brownstone way possible.

Tricking the army of hitmen onto Camp Pendleton had been flashy enough, but his frontal assault on the Harriken headquarters had surprised even her—and she'd already seen what he could do.

The authorities had only made it more spectacular by issuing a rare organizational bounty.

It was just like she'd predicted. The damned Harriken wouldn't leave him alone, so he'd ended them in America.

*Learned your lesson yet, or does he need to come over to Japan and finish you off?*

At least things were over and Alison would be safe.

Her gaze roamed the room. Two men at a table in the center caught her attention and made the hairs on the back of her neck stand up, but she couldn't figure out why.

*What am I missing?*

The men, both sipping beers, chatted quietly. There was nothing unusual about them, but something about the way they carried themselves insinuated itself into the back of her mind and wouldn't go away.

The ex-killer pulled out her phone and held it up like she was going to take a selfie, but she made sure to angle the phone so the two men would be in the shot. After snapping the picture, she forwarded it to Peyton and sent him a quick text.

**Need to know if these guys are trouble ASAP.**

Shay returned to sipping her drink and only occasionally glanced around the bar to verify the men were still there.

---

Everybody had a camera, and every modern city was filled with drones. A lot of people didn't remember that, or even if they did, they didn't seem to care.

That made it hard to hide, even with magic. That was why Peyton and Shay had both needed to "die" rather than just move. If anyone knew to look for them, they'd be screwed.

Peyton considered those truths as he isolated the faces

from Shay's picture and adjusted the lighting to make it easier for his facial recognition algorithms to work.

He smiled. He might not be able to cook pizza worth a damn, but this kind of work was trivial for him. Even the great Shay Carson needed his help.

A check of public criminal databases wasn't turning anything up, so he brought up a program that linked him to a few sketchier underworld databases. Even scumbags and criminals appreciated the value of collating data and having it accessible via a convenient API. The trick was mostly knowing who to pay to get access to that sort of thing.

His computer beeped; he'd found a match in seconds.

"Damn I'm good." He brought up the record. "Ah, that explains why it popped up so quickly. They're the kind of scumbags who want to pretend they aren't."

Bryce Smith and John Southward, both sergeants with Grayson Private Military Contracting Services.

There were a lot of PMC companies all over the world with different levels of repute, but the Grayson crew were nothing more than vicious mercenaries who didn't care who hired them as long as they got paid.

They also happened to be the company that lost dozens of men in the raid on Belmont House. It hadn't been Brownstone's fault, but they didn't know that. It wasn't like Shay or Brownstone, at least as far as Peyton knew, had gone out of their way to clarify that.

Angry mercenaries hanging out in the same city as Alison struck Peyton as the very definition of trouble.

**Both those guys are with Grayson PMC Services.**

**Thanks, Peyton. That's helpful.**

Shay sighed. The coincidence of two Grayson mercenaries being in a bar close to the School for Necessary Magic with a picture of Alison was too great to ignore.

*How the fuck did they get a picture of Alison? Not good.*

Twenty minutes later the men got up to leave, and Shay rose and headed to the front while they were still standing over their table. She hurried out of the bar and peeked into a nearby alley. The security camera near the end might make things difficult for her.

"Hey, guys," she called, fluttering her eyelashes and speaking in that higher pitch again. "I drank...a lot tonight." She ran a hand up her side. "I'm Stephanie. What are your names?"

"I'm John," one of the men offered.

"Kendrik," the other chimed in.

Shay leaned forward and took a deep breath. A low-cut dress rather than a T-shirt and leather jacket might have been helpful right about then, but acting would have to make up for it. She locked eyes with Kendrik.

John shrugged. "We can do the other thing tomorrow. Not like the girl's going anywhere."

*You're damn right Alison's not going anywhere.*

Shay sashayed into the alley, and the two grinning men hurried after her.

When they were out of view of the street, Shay reached into her back pocket and gestured for John and Kendrik to come closer.

Both men stepped forward, eager for what she was offering.

Shay pulled out a stiletto switchblade and pressed the button, and the blade extended with a click.

A minute later, she pulled out a small case. She considered leaving her card on the bodies, but decided not to.

"No. They'll just have to wonder."

S hay tossed the cell phone she'd recovered in Hokkaido
on Peyton's desk. "That's my present for you. I went
all the way to Japan to get it."

Peyton eyed her with suspicion. "I already have a
phone. I *like* my phone."

She rolled her eyes. "It's the phone I grabbed from those
assholes on the Ainu job. You said you could crack it."

"Oh, almost forgot. Yeah, that'll be easy." He snorted.
"Give me something hard to do."

"Do you need something harder? Wouldn't want you to
get bored and start ordering more random shit for the
warehouse. Maybe I can send you after Snegurka."

"What about Snegurka?" Lily came in, busy sticking a
pen inside of her cast, trying to scratch an itch. "I can't wait
to get this thing off. What about the Ice Witch? Has she
been spotted again?"

"Easy, Lily. I haven't forgotten about your quest. Peyton
thinks cracking the phone is too easy for him. You want to
take a stab at it?"

Peyton grinned and waved his hands in front of his face. "No, no. It's fine. I love it when things are easy. I'll do it."

"Good. Now that Brownstone's not going to be attacked for five seconds, I can concentrate on being a tomb raider again."

"Can you believe what happened? The guy took on an entire building by himself." Peyton shook his head. "If I was on his bad side, I think I'd just shoot myself rather than face him. That guy's like a force of nature."

Shay snickered. "Yeah, the man does kick a lot of ass when he wants to, which seems to be a lot lately."

"When do I get to meet the myth?" Lily sat on the couch, crossing her legs underneath.

"Not yet."

"Let me do the Shay to English translation for you," said Peyton. "He doesn't know you exist yet."

Shay flicked the side of Peyton's head, eliciting a yelp. "Soon-ish." Shay bit her lip, trying to figure out how to ease a teenager into a new idea. Blurt it out might work. "What would you think about going to a fancy boarding school for kids your age with magical abilities? Fresh air, no danger, hone your skills, make friends."

"No, no and no."

"Well, at least she thought about it carefully," said Peyton, who ducked at the sight of Shay's cold, steely glare. "Backing out of conversation now."

"You would make an even better tomb raider."

"Adult lie number one. I'll make a better tomb raider hanging out here. This is my trade school."

"What if I ordered you to go?"

"I'd run away and become your competition a little earlier than planned."

Shay let out a snort as Peyton rolled his eyes and slowly backed across the room, finding something to do around the pizza oven.

"You're years away from giving me a run for any of my money."

"Still running away and we'd see. I'm not going. This was the deal we made and either you abide by our agreed terms or you made a deal in bad faith." Lily set her jaw, standing up from the couch and her one good arm on her hip.

But Shay saw the tears in her eyes. The kid thinks I'm done with her. "Forget I mentioned it. It was a half-baked idea. You're right. Trade school."

Lily wiped her face with her sleeve, her jaw still set.

That probably set us back a bit, thought Shay.

"I wonder if Brownstone uses any sort of magical items?" Peyton furrowed his brow, walking back into the fray, doing his best to change the subject. "You've worked with him. What kind of equipment does he have?"

"Not really sure." Shay shrugged. She glanced over at Lily and even took a step toward her to try a hug, but the girl backed away. Maybe tomorrow.

It was a half-truth. She *didn't* know much about the amulet. She knew what it did, but she didn't know the nature of its magic or the source of its power.

Brownstone had his reasons for using the item in front of her, and it spoke to the trust he had in her. The existence of the amulet wasn't her information to pass along to anyone just yet. If Peyton got pissy about it later, she'd tell him as much. It wasn't like she was going to Brownstone and telling him Peyton's life story.

"And that Marine thing!" Peyton whistled. "Damn. How does a guy even plan something like that? Would *you* have thought of something like that?"

Shay smirked. "I doubt I could have gotten a bunch of Marines to help me, but it doesn't matter. It looks like we got ourselves a Brownstone fanboy." She smiled and looked at Lily, but she had wandered into the office and her back was turned.

Shay patted the phone. "Get this unlocked, and maybe I'll get you his autograph."

"Ha-ha. Very funny. I'm just saying I respect his skills."

"Not saying I don't." Shay shrugged. "Just keep in mind, Brownstone's a bounty hunter. He doesn't have the… checkered past we do."

"I don't really have a checkered past. It's mostly just my brother trying to kill me."

"Brownstone doesn't have to hide, is all I'm saying. It's good for us both to remember the position we're in." She nodded to the phone. "And you've got work to do."

Peyton nodded. "Yeah, I do." He walked off, shoulders slumped.

Shay sighed. *Great, I've pissed off everyone today. I win. Is there a grownup around to hang with? Where's that damn cat?*

She believed everything she'd said, but she was trying to convince herself as much as Peyton.

*Get out of my head, Brownstone.*

A half-hour later Peyton marched up to Shay with a shit-eating grin on his face. "I've got good news."

"There's a half-off sale on loud suits at the mall?"

Peyton shook his head. "I wish. Nope. I've got the identification on the phone. It belongs to Hollingsworth Retrieval Specialists."

Shay frowned. "I've heard of them. They're based out of England. They aren't known for being ruthless assholes or anything, but they *are* known for being damned reckless."

"I'll say. They got themselves blown up. That's pretty reckless."

The tomb raider chuckled. "Yeah. This isn't the first time they've lost a team on a job." She frowned. "Though I wonder why their name wasn't more public on this one. They don't usually hide when they are on a job. Find anything else that might be useful?"

"I've already copied the data off the phone, but they've got good operational security. They received calls from numbers associated with their company, but there's not a lot stored on the phone. I'm surprised they'd be so careful about everything else and then just call from an easily-traceable number."

Shay snorted. "Like I said, they don't usually hide. They don't have to. Not every tomb raider is a former killer who faked her death and helped a hacker fake his, and not everyone has to be as careful about hiding their identities as we are."

"Good point."

"Looks like the job's back on. I'll let the Professor know we've got a lead and see how he wants to play this."

Shay expected several different responses, but not the one she actually received.

"Just stop looking, Miz Carson."

She pulled her phone back to stare at it for a second before putting it back to her ear. "Huh? Did you just tell me to stop looking?"

"I did. I think you should abort this job, and since I'm the one paying you can pretty much consider that an order." He chuckled. "If you want to recover it yourself, that's fine, but I won't pay for it."

"But I've got a lead. I thought this carving was a big deal. You seemed hell-bent on getting it fast before."

"It was indeed a big deal at the time I hired you. It's no longer something worthy of attention. For various reasons, I'm no longer interested in the modulator. You can keep all the money I've already paid you."

Shay gritted her teeth. "It doesn't have to go down this way. I can still find it, Professor."

Smite-Williams let out a merry laugh. "Oh, don't worry, Miz Carson. I've got something else I'm more interested in acquiring soon, and I can't think of anyone else I'd rather have looking for it. I'm just working out a few more of the details before I ask you to commit. I'll be in touch soon, Miz Carson."

"You're sure about the carving?"

"Quite. I'll even help you out by letting you know pursuing it would be a waste of your time, even if you desire an artifact for your private collection."

Shay took a deep breath. "Understood."

"Now, if you'll excuse me, I have a few things to take care of." He hung up.

*Probably a few beers to take care of. More than a few.*

The Professor wasn't pissed and wanted to hire her again, which meant she didn't have to worry about another hit to her reputation. But between the carving and the magic beans, that was two recent jobs she hadn't completed after a string of complete successes.

Pride, more than concern, ruled her now. It wasn't good enough to be a mere tomb raider. She wanted to be the person clients thought of when they even said the word.

*Damn it. I'd still go after it, but he made it sound like it's lost its power.*

Smite-Williams might have been wrong when he'd said it was still in existence. After the crater she'd witnessed in Japan, she wouldn't be surprised if the artifact were nothing but ash in the Hokkaido wind. That didn't make her feel any better.

Danger was easy to deal with. Disappointment was harder to swallow.

Shay snickered and shook her head. She needed to pull her head out of her ass. She was going to have to learn to be Zen about tomb raiding if she were going to last.

---

*This is a bad idea. This is the worst fucking idea he's ever had. I shouldn't be feeding into his ridiculous male ego. Some things are not meant to be trifled with just because a man convinces himself he's tough enough to handle it.*

Shay paced as Peyton's stupid grin kept growing. Lily had finally come out of the office and was cautiously sitting nearby on the edge of a chair, waiting to see what magic came out of the oven.

Peyton stood in front of his pizza oven, his apron splotched with both fresh stains and darker ones that looked days old.

Scorch marks covered the front of his oven.

"Just how much pizza did you make when I was gone?" Shay inquired. "Or were you just throwing grenades around here for fun? New game with Lily maybe?"

Peyton snatched his paddle from the table and slipped it under his latest creation. "Just a little here and there. I bought the oven to use it. It's not a decoration." He set the pizza on a tray. "I'll admit that you were right—making good pizza is about a lot more than just the oven. I'm humble enough to accept that."

"Oh, you think?" Shay rolled her eyes. "So wise. I kneel before your great sagacity."

Lily was chewing on the end of her sleeve, doing her best imitation of bored but Shay already knew better. She was dying to get into it with Peyton.

Peyton raised his index finger. "But I've had time to practice, you see. Now I understand my proportions, flavor profile, temperatures, and toppings." He nodded as if he were trying to convince himself as much as her. "And I've improved. I've been focusing on the sauce. I think that's key.

"I shopped around to get just the right tomatoes. It's all about proper acid balance and the soil. I had to hit up few different farmer's markets to find what I wanted, but it'll all be worth it once you taste this fine pie. You'll regret ever doubting me."

"That's good to hear." Shay nodded approvingly. "I'll even say it sounds like you've finally bought a clue. There may be some small hope for you to make something that isn't totally disgusting." She held her thumb and forefinger together. "Just a tiny amount."

"Get ready to be as impressed as you ever have been by the actions of a single man."

Shay laughed.

Peyton sliced the pizza and set a piece on a plate. He handed it to Shay, an eager and expectant look on his face.

*He* did *say he had been practicing. How bad could it be?*

Shay took a bite and swallowed hard. She walked to the garbage can, tossed in the slice, and marched toward her Fiat with a grimace on her face.

*What the fuck was that, anti-pizza?*

"If you're going out for pizza, I want pepperoni on mine," Peyton yelled.

She shook her head as she threw open the driver door. Behind her, she heard Lily let out a laugh and Shay felt a smile grow across her face. Damn, it's not easy raising a teenager, even in a makeshift trade school.

The would-be pizza maker poured himself a glass of cabernet.

"Hey, at least the wine's good." Lily let out another laugh and said, "Pour me a glass."

"No!" yelled Shay.

Shay slammed the door and started her car. The wine was probably vinegar. The pizza had certainly tasted like it.

A few days later, Shay leaned against the wall of Warehouse Two with her arms crossed and a huge frown on her face. The night before had been good. Damned good. After not seeing Brownstone for a while, she'd gone out to dinner at a decent place with the man, his idea to repay her for her keeping an eye on Alison. It almost had the feeling of a date, at least on her end.

Brownstone had been as clueless as ever, and Shay decided to not worry about it. She respected the man, and he respected her. That was enough for now, even if she was willing to admit she might like to try for something more.

*That's on him. I'm not gonna chase him like some lonely teen. I still don't how much of this is about him not noticing me.*

But this morning it had all come crashing down on her. Her previous life hadn't involved her having to manage anyone, so the concept of dealing with an assistant who was late was novel in an annoying way. Lily looked up amused from where she sat, waiting to see what Shay would do next.

"Threatening to shoot him probably won't motivate him in the way you want," she said with a smirk.

Shay tapped her fingers against her arms. She could burn down Peyton's new place when he wasn't there and make it look like an accident. That might force him back into the warehouse with Lily, but it wouldn't last.

Shay shook her head. That kind of thinking was too much of the old Killer Shay, and not enough kinder, gentler Tomb Raider Shay. At least, kinder and gentler in the sense she'd only break your knees instead of killing you if she had a choice.

Peyton was a great assistant in many ways, and he had useful skills, even if making pizza wasn't among them. A touch more professionalism wouldn't hurt, though. She needed to figure out how to instill it in him without ruining his creativity and motivation.

The loading bay door slid up and Peyton drove a van inside. He threw open the door and rushed over to her. "Sorry I'm late. I was just trying a new strategy to evade tails."

"Oh? And what's that? You drive the longest, most-complicated route possible?"

Peyton shook his head. "It's this technique where I use a random number generator to decide if I'm going to go left or right at Hillhurst Avenue, so that changes the entire rest of my route. Then I use it at a different intersection, like Tallmadge and Finley, and that changes things. It's kind of a nested thing. I randomly determine which intersection to change course."

"Uh-huh, and I should care because…"

He threw his hands in the air. "Because it always ends up being a roundabout way from my place to here, but since so many key parts of it are random it's not like anyone could learn my route. It's all but perfect because even *I* don't know what route I'm going to take."

Shay just glared at the man, more annoyed by his tardiness than impressed by his technique, even if she *could* see the advantages.

She nodded toward the office. "Your computer has been

going nuts with alerts. I was gonna look at it, but I kept thinking that some other person should be here to do that."

"I offered," Lily raised her good arm in the air.

"Some guy who is supposed to be my research assistant and computer specialist is supposed to do it."

"Oh, yeah. I know. I have it hooked up to my phone so I can check from anywhere."

"But you won't work from home?"

Peyton shrugged. "I said I don't like to work from home, but don't worry, the point is I have you covered 24/7."

"Something I also mentioned. Just sayin'," said Lily. She bit into a cold Pop-Tart, shrugging her shoulders.

"Oh cinnamon, snap. That was mine, wasn't it," said Peyton. "No bigs. I can share."

"Okay. What's the big alert?"

"A new job. Since the Professor still hasn't contacted you about the next job, I've been poking around a little looking for work." Peyton gestured toward the door. "I figure, you know, it's time to get back out there again. Back on the horse, regain that momentum, and all that."

Shay rolled her eyes. "I don't need a pep talk, especially from you."

"I'm not saying you do, but I also think you're a little pissy still about Antarctica and Hokkaido."

Shay shot her most murderous glare at Peyton. He needed to shut his mouth before she shut it for him.

Peyton held up his hand. "Okay, let's just forget about that. The point is, there's a new job, and you didn't mention not taking any new ones. Or am I wrong?"

"No, I didn't." Shay softened her expression. "I'm listening. Tell me about the job."

He waited a few seconds before continuing, "It's in Edirne, Turkey. There's an ancient stone there. Two feet by one foot."

"Please tell me it's not filled with mysterious symbols we don't understand. There's only so much of that I can take right now."

Peyton shook his head. "Nope. This isn't a mystery, it's just good old-fashioned magic. Well, sort of."

"Sort of?"

"It's magic, but also like the manual to magic. It's got an inscription in ancient Hittite that's the beginning of a spell to extend life. Not sure if the stone is necessary for the magic, but it is supposed to have some magic power."

Shay nodded. "It always comes back to immortality."

"Yeah, according to my research, there are several of these stones all over the world, all with inscriptions, all different ancient languages, all part of the same spell."

"Huh. That's different," said Lily.

"Yep. There are rumored to be nine. No one has ever found them all, and the few that have been found have gone missing again through the years. Only that one in Hittite and another in ancient Chinese have been verified to still exist in the last hundred years." Peyton pointed toward his computer. "The stone in Turkey has been missing since 1938, but now it's been found again."

Shay crossed her arms. "And you're sure the stone's there?"

"Everything suggests it is, and the client is willing to pay a lot of money for you to recover it. He specifically was looking to hire you. Well, Aletheia." Peyton shrugged. "He wants someone with experience working with dangerous artifacts, but he claims all you need to do to prevent the stone from exhibiting any magic power is to seal it in an airtight bag. The archaeologists who found it won't move it because they're concerned about dangers."

*Yeah, like artifacts blowing a crater into a hillside.*

"I'll make sure to bring a bag." She frowned. "You mentioned a specific city. I'm not an expert on Turkish geography. Is this some necropolis in the middle of nowhere?"

"Nope, it's a living, if ancient, city. The stone's actually in a recently-unearthed burial mound on the edge."

"Does anyone else know about it?"

Lily opened her mouth to say something as Shay held up her hand. "I wasn't going to ask if I could come along. Only have the one wing," she said, waving her cast. "I was going to ask *Peyton* if I could help *him*."

Peyton gave a crooked smile, and gave her a nod. "I can find enough to keep you busy."

"Now that we have that settled, I'll ask again. Does anyone else know about it?"

Peyton shook his head. "Nope. Best I can tell, the stone was uncovered in the last few days. The client seemed very interested in getting it away from the city as soon as possible. Basically, if you're not willing to commit to recovery within the next seventy-two hours, there's no deal."

Shay laughed. "Eager beaver. Maybe that shit explodes after a few days."

A little tension lined Peyton's face. "Now for the bad news."

"Bad news? It does explode?"

"I don't know about that, but my research found a lot of unusual deaths associated with people who've found these stones. Not just deaths, violent deaths."

"A curse?"

He shrugged. "Don't know. Mangled bodies, though. Many hacked into pieces."

"Sounds less like a curse and more like someone took them out."

"Maybe, but if you just grab it, I'm sure it won't be a big deal. I hope." Peyton clapped once. "You know what? What am I worried about? You can handle a few thugs. I'm sure it'll be an easy jo—"

The tomb raider cut him off with a glare. There were no such things as easy jobs, just jobs that had more opportunity to turn into clusterfucks. She'd known that even as a killer, and she'd let herself forget until the snow bitch had shown up and stolen her damned magic beans.

Shay gestured at Peyton. "You just got done telling me about hacked-up and mangled bodies."

"Yeah, but those were all people who didn't know about actual magic like you. You'll be ready if anything weird happens, and if it's just thugs, you can take them down. You'll be prepared. You've killed a lot of people...and, well, *things*." Peyton shrugged. "The client is willing to pay a lot of money, including a huge deposit. Maybe it won't be easy or maybe it will, but I think it's a good job."

"Yeah, it *sounds* like a good job, and it's good to hear that my rep wasn't hurt too badly by Antarctica."

"See? No one blames you for getting iced." Peyton shot

a stupid grin at Lily who mouthed, *run*. "A vision?" he asked.

Shay pulled out her gun.

Peyton blinked. "What are you doing?"

"Checking to see if it's loaded."

"Fair enough. Let's change the subject."

Lily let out a whoop of laughter and ran over to Shay, wrapping her arms around her in a hug. Teenagers, thought Shay, startled, hugging her back as she held the gun away from her.

L ater that evening, Shay strolled into Warehouse Four, humming. Peyton's information checked out on initial review, but she wanted to hit her library sources to see if she could find out anything else. Her gut told her there was something else to this stone and the life spell she should know about, if only because of the elaborate separation of the incantation into nine different sections.

That suggested someone wanted to preserve the magic but didn't want anyone using it. Given how old the two known stones were, that was an impressive feat and might indicate Oriceran involvement.

From what Shay had seen, magic was a lot like most technologies. No one wanted to give up the power to manipulate reality once they'd achieved it, even if it caused a lot of problems.

Shay moved through the stacks toward a small section on Hittite history. The ancient Anatolian people might not have anything to do with the creation of the artifact, but it was a good place to start.

The tomb raider let out a sigh. It was a narrow slice of books in the huge personal library, but that section happened to be at the top of one of her wall shelves.

A quick trip across the room netted her one of her rolling ladders. Once she'd reached the top, she realized she'd miscalculated on the position of the book she wanted. Instead of climbing back down, she swung across the bolted shelf, snagged the book, and returned to the ladder.

"There we go."

Shay smiled and headed toward a small cozy nook she'd set up in a side room. With its comfortable lounge chair and soft lighting it was a relaxing place to review a tome or two, just not the place for stacks of books and pages of furious note-scribbling.

Shay settled into the soft leather chair. Tomb raiding was about money, first and foremost, but it was also about her love of history, and it was nights like this she could appreciate that.

She planned to leave for Turkey bright and early the next morning, but a few hours of reading would not only be useful, it'd also relax her.

*Let's see what I can dig up.*

---

The tomb raider stifled a yawn. She was on her third book in as many hours. Surveying the ancient Anatolian culture of the Hittites was interesting, but it had yet to give her any insights that might help on the job. She'd vowed to check out one last work, a translated copy of a

1945 German book, *The Secret Occult History of the Bronze Age.*

Shay was ready to head home when a footnote caught her eye.

*Wolf agrees with Klein that the proper translation of the text of the temple inscription mentioned in Klein's survey would be more properly rendered as "denying death" rather than "extending life." (Wolf 24)*

The rest of the chapter mainly discussed issues with the translation of ancient languages and didn't mention anything else that could be construed as having anything to do with the stone.

Even if the tidbit had anything to do with the stone she was looking for, it didn't matter. Shay wasn't planning on collecting the nine stones and achieving immortality, either by "denying death" or "extending life," whatever the difference was.

Shay stretched and yawned. "Time to grab me an artifact."

---

Men choked the streets, all streaming toward colorful banners in the distance. Many walked without shirts, their toned muscles on display under the morning sun. They chatted jovially in Turkish. She doubted anything they were saying was important enough she should use machine translation. Few paid her much attention.

She smirked to herself. The universe had a sense of humor after all. She'd hit the city during its famed annual oil-wrestling tournament. If she hadn't been there on a job, she might have taken in a few rounds of greased-up men rolling around with each other. The simple pleasures made life bearable.

An image of a shirtless and oiled Brownstone popped into her head. Even if he didn't notice her, it didn't change the fact he was the Grand Master of Six Packs. She had most definitely noticed *that*.

Shay shook her head. Respect for Brownstone was flowing together with admiration of some of his other traits more often than not lately.

The tomb raider pushed out the thought of oiled bounty hunters and moved up the street, her gaze sweeping the area. She was careful not to make eye contact with any of the men. She didn't want or need to draw any attention to herself.

Her current outfit, a robe and a head scarf, was opposite on the modesty scale from the shirtless men. She'd chosen it to keep a lower profile and hide her identity, but she was impressed by how many weapons she could hide under the robe. She could have probably hidden the Masamune *tachi* under it. Shay snickered at the thought.

The street was almost as thick with tourists who'd shown up to take in the festival celebrating all things oily and virile. More people to give her cover—which was good.

Her mirth vanished as she turned a corner. Four minarets rose in the distance, surrounding the massive dome and three balconies of the Selimiye Mosque.

*Okay, nothing like a building older than your country to give you some perspective.*

She wasn't there to sightsee. Not entirely, anyway.

Getting a firsthand look at the street layout might help her later if she needed to beat a hasty retreat.

A few more minutes of sightseeing and escape planning brought her to a small café. She pushed inside and winced as a powerful smell ambushed her and brought bile to her throat.

People who didn't travel much took for granted sensory familiarity and how challenges to that could push a person off-balance, especially smell—one of the more evocative of the senses. Shay sucked in a breath and focused.

The scent was hard to identify at first. It reminded her of a combination of rust and blood, but her review of local culture on the plane en route helped her figure out the source sitting on several plates—cigercisi, or fried calf's liver.

Shay wasn't anemic enough to try to eat something like that.

The din attacked her ears as the cigercisi went after her nose.

Several large groups of men sat around tables making boisterous declarations—judging by the tone—and pounded down drinks in a distinctly un-Islamic display of alcohol consumption.

Whiffs of anise suggested everyone was drinking *raki*.

*You don't get much more Turkish than this place, so the coffee's gonna be authentic. That's a win.*

Now it was just a test to see if she could tolerate the smell long enough to acquire the drink.

Shay was always insulted by a poor tail. The two obvious plainclothes Turkish cops who'd been following her since her stop at the café didn't even bother to wipe the looks of concentration off their faces.

She'd give them credit for sensing she might be a troublemaker, considering all the people, Turkish or otherwise, who were there for the festival.

Thankfully, the city's skies weren't as choked with drones as LA or New York. Once she lost the cops, she'd be able to make her way to the burial mound site at the edge of the city with ease.

The sun hung low on the western horizon. She'd have a good chance to escape soon if she timed it right.

Shay made her way toward the thickening crowds flowing toward the mosque. She walked with a steady but not quick pace. The cops didn't need to know she was on to them. The minutes passed as she closed on the mosque.

A loud, sonorous Arabic chant erupted from the mosque. The call to prayer echoed through the nearby streets and alleys. A ripple of interest passed through the crowds as they headed toward the mosque.

The two cops following Shay took their attention off her for a moment and focused on the mosque.

*And you'd been doing so well, guys. Too bad. Big mistake.*

The tomb raider ducked into an alley and broke into a sprint. She checked over her shoulder as she hit the exit. No tailing cops in sight.

*Sorry, but I've got a job to do.*

Shay stepped out of her gray rental Fiat Qubo. The ultra-compact minivan wasn't the type of vehicle she wanted to drive, but it didn't stand out and wouldn t be all that suspicious driving by the fenced area surrounding the mound site.

Her jammers would keep any drones out of the area, and she didn't see much in the way of security other than the fence.

She'd switched out of her robe and into a loaded tactical harness, jacket, pants, and boots. She also put on a headlamp. She wasn't sure what to expect, but the job smelled too easy to her—and Peyton's warnings about mangled bodies ensured she wouldn't let her guard down.

*Damn it. Maybe I should have brought the magic sword after all.*

Shay carefully made her way toward the burial mound. She heard something scratching and dropped to her knees behind a pile of crates, fishing out a sonic grenade. A little shock and awe might be enough to get her through and to the stone.

She poked her head around the corner. Unless she really misunderstood anatomy, a sonic grenade wouldn't work.

*Well, fuck. I guess I know the difference between extending life and denying death now.*

Half a dozen animated skeletons wandered back and forth in front of the excavated entrance. They all held curved single-edged sabers and small elaborately-decorated round shields, pre-modern Ottoman-era equipment.

The blades gleamed in the moonlight, not a hint of dust or rust on them. The shields looked as if they'd been painted the day before. They didn't resemble equipment pulled from a burial mound.

*What the fuck is up with the undead lately? Overpopulation at its worst. Motherfucking skeletons.*

Shay decided the only thing worse than a zombie was a damned skeleton. At least a zombie still had organs a person might target. Their anatomy and movement made sense—magical, but not too magical.

Everything about a moving skeleton was a mockery of biology and physics. They were pure magic in the most annoying sense. Shooting a walking pile of bones with a pistol was pointless.

*Now I really wish I'd brought the sword. Maybe it'd be great at chopping skeletons up. First, though, I've got to figure out how these bone assholes hunt.*

Shay grabbed a rock and threw it against the metal casing of an unpowered spotlight. The rock clinked and fell to the ground. The skeletons ignored it.

*Okay, so not sound. How do I get past them? Just walk?*

Shay unsheathed one of her adamantine knives and crept toward the skeletons, holding her breath. A few seconds passed, and the skeletons continued to wander near the mound.

The stupid things couldn't even see her. Of course they couldn't; they didn't have eyes. She let out a sigh of relief. They were just for show.

All of the skeletons spun toward her and advanced.

"Well, shit. Fuck it." Shay ducked a saber. The skeletons rushed after her, not able to match her speed but not lumbering like zombies either.

She slashed with her knife, but other than nicking the

bone, she didn't accomplish much. The skeleton didn't react at all.

Shay pulled out a second knife in time to parry a powerful slash from a different skeleton. For bastards with no muscles, they hit hard.

The force of the blows pushed her back. She slashed again and again with her knives, but her enemies weren't reacting to her hits and scratching up bones wasn't a great way to win a fight against something already dead.

Shay blocked another blow and considered her options. A frag grenade wouldn't have enough force to blow apart bones.

*Am I gonna have to start carrying C4 everywhere with me?*

Shay snorted. *I wonder if this is how Brownstone felt when he fought those zombies?*

The armed piles of bones spread out in a half-circle. A few quick dodges saved Shay from some nasty lacerations, but she was running out of room to maneuver.

*Fuck it. I'm not leaving without my damned stone.*

The tomb raider flipped on her headlamp and rushed into the burial mound. A saber whizzed by, missing her neck by mere inches.

The excavation had followed the original contours of the long-decayed walls that had once separated the low-ceilinged chambers.

The only noise as she rushed forward was her heavy breathing and the scratching of the bony feet behind her. She would have preferred a few groans or moans.

*How do the bastards even sense me?*

The skeletons hadn't reacted to the noise of the rock or seeing her at first. She didn't understand how they detected her. Maybe, like Alison, they could sense souls at close ranges or something similar. Magic tended to make sense in its own weird way.

Something clicked in her head. Shay spun toward the advancing skeletons, her mind afire with sudden understanding. Everything made perfect sense.

*Airtight bag, huh?*

She held her breath.

The skeletons stopped and turned back to the entrance.

The tomb raider grinned to herself as she hurried down the thin path between a few of the sub-chambers toward the main burial chamber lying at the end.

The stone lay in the center of the chamber, alone. She wasn't sure if it'd been buried that way originally, or if other objects had been already removed. If the archaeologists had any inkling of what the stone did they might have been too afraid to move it.

Shay's lungs started to burn. She sucked in a deep breath and waited, her blades raised. The skeletons didn't invade the mound.

"Guess you guys are patient as long as I'm not close? I can deal with that."

She removed a folded silver bag with a small plastic air valve on the side. She placed the stone inside and sealed the bag using its own adhesive strip before removing a small electric pump from her bag. The tomb raider connected the pump to the bag and evacuated all the air.

"Hope this vacuum-sealing shit works."

Shay took another deep breath and held it before running toward the entrance.

No skeletons waited for her, none standing anyway.

Instead, piles of bones lay around the entrance, their swords and shields gone.

Shay let out the breath and took several more. She let a huge smile spread on her face on her way to the minivan.

*An easy job or two never hurts.*

Peyton stifled a yawn as he watched his computer. A message popped up from Shay.

**Not an easy job. Locals on the lookout for archaeological site vandal, but no description of me or my rental vehicle. Should have left last night instead of waiting. Too hot to extract from here. Gonna drive to Athens. Take care of my flight. Look after Lily.**

"Easy for you to say," Peyton muttered, yawning again.

Shay might be driving around Turkey in the middle of the afternoon, but the time-zone difference meant Peyton was dealing with a late night.

The researcher sighed and brought up the reservation website. Another yawn attack hit him. He needed to get to bed soon.

If he finished up in the next few minutes, it'd still take a long time to get home. It wasn't a quick drive even as a straight shot, and the required circuitous safety route would only make it longer. Dying in a car accident after escaping a hit wasn't his idea of a good ending.

A folded-up cot near the office caught his attention and called to him. He might have torn down most of the cubicle maze, but it wouldn't hurt to spend a night in the warehouse even if the cot was uncomfortable.

*See, Shay? You're getting your wish.*

Peyton smiled. He'd been working hard, and Shay would be fine once he made the reservations and she flew out of Athens.

Shay would probably hit Warehouse Five to drop off the artifact and worry about setting up the drop the next day. Between all the travel and logistics, Peyton could easily squeeze in a night off.

*An apartment's one thing and a pet's another, but it's time to really start living again. Not like Shay needs to know about everything I do. She doesn't tell me everything* she *does. Lily can take care of herself and insists on doing so, anyway.*

He smiled. Everything was going to turn out all right.

---

*Thanks, Shay. Thanks a lot.*

The next evening, Peyton adjusted his phone earpiece as he stepped into the crowded bar. Shay had made it to Athens without trouble, but her flight had been delayed and now the Greek authorities were also on the lookout for the "stolen important historical artifact." Everyone in that region was suddenly getting along just in time to screw the tomb raider.

Peyton divided his time between scanning the crowd and glancing at his phone for updates. Shay's poor timing had become his poor timing.

*This is what I get for convincing myself I'd have an open night without any worries about Shay.*

Lily was tucked into bed in the warehouse with an iPad and enough downloaded movies to keep her up till dawn and a freezer full of ice cream. The girl wasn't going anywhere. Peyton congratulated himself on his ingenuity.

Still, Shay was the unknown factor.

Meeting a girl from the Hello Cupid dating site at a bar might be a bad idea, given his current life situation. He was sure Shay would say as much, but he didn't care.

He was tired of living in the shadows. Shay and Peyton were both supposed to be dead, but she had a life. She had friends and jaunted around the country and world. For that matter, she got to hang out with a muscle-bound badass like Brownstone. Peyton didn't know if they had anything going on, but he found it hard to believe a woman wouldn't find a guy like that at least a little attractive. He was the Conan to her Red Sonja.

All Peyton had was a cat. A nice cat, but still just a cat and a pseudo little sister.

He could be just as careful as the tomb raider. If asking permission wouldn't work he'd ask forgiveness later, or better yet, just not get caught.

Peyton looked up from his phone. A cute blonde in silver glasses and a black dress waved from a table in the corner.

*Wow. She looks even better in person.*

He was rocking an awesome blue seersucker suit, but he hadn't used a profile picture, figuring it'd be too risky to let free into the net. He was surprised the woman even agreed to meet.

Peyton made his way over to the woman. "Tricia?"

"Peyton?"

"Surprise." He held out his hand.

Tricia smiled and shook his hand. "It's so nice to meet you, Peyton. You're a lot cuter than I imagined." She gasped and put a hand over her mouth. "That sounded rude."

He took a seat and winked. "Not going to complain about someone saying they like how I look."

Peyton's phone vibrated and he pulled it out for a quick glance.

**Might be trouble. Might not be. I'll let you know.**

The arrival of the waitress saved Peyton from groaning at his phone. He was half-convinced Shay was screwing him over on purpose while she sipped wine in a hotel room somewhere rather than desperately trying to avoid the attention of authorities in Greece.

"I'll have a glass of cabernet."

Tricia smiled. "Funny. That's exactly what I was going to order." She winked.

"I'll have that right to you," the waitress replied.

Peyton laughed. "Guess the site was right about our compatibility."

"Yeah. Oh, I just wanted to tell you, I love your sense of fashion. It's so bold and memorable."

"Thanks. I try." He shrugged.

*See, Shay? Some people appreciate my look.*

"It's one of my passions, actually. I work in an office right now, but I have my own online company where I sell clothes I design."

"A fashion designer? Nice."

Tricia's cheeks reddened. "I don't know if I'm comfortable calling myself that yet, but I do design clothes."

"Why didn't you mention any of that on your profile?"

The conversation stopped as the waitress delivered their drinks. "Ready to order?"

Tricia and Peyton both shook their head.

"I'll be back in a few minutes then." The waitress departed.

Tricia took a sip of her drink before speaking again. "I didn't want to seem pretentious and scare you off, but once I got here and saw you, I knew everything would work out. You've got a good air. I feel like I can be honest with you."

*Wish I could say the same, Tricia.*

"That's cool." Peyton smiled.

"What about you? You just said you were in IT?"

"I work for a tech start-up, actually." Peyton took a sip of his wine. Easy lies came with his lifestyle both before and after his "death."

Tricia's eyes widened. "Really? You're going to be a billionaire someday?"

"Probably not. It's all...you know, a bit more limited. It involves providing organizational software for charities. Not very sexy."

"I don't know about sexy, but that's impressive. You sound like you're really making a difference."

*Wonder what she'd think if she knew I helped Shay in a tomb-raider business. Collecting artifacts makes a difference. Maybe not a good one all the time, but a difference.*

"Okay, have to move fast," Shay barked, her breathing heavy. "Confirm the flight number for me. I can't look at my phone so just tell me."

It took Peyton a few seconds to realize it wasn't Tricia talking.

He forced a smile. "I'm really sorry, but my phone just buzzed. My boss has me on call…you know, 24/7, so I just have to check on this real quick."

Tricia blinked. "O-okay."

Peyton sighed and brought his phone up to his mouth.

"What's the flight number?" Shay hissed into his earpiece. Something thudded in the background and a loud groan followed.

"What was that?" Peyton inquired.

"Don't worry. He didn't see my face, and he's not dead."

"He's not… Okay."

"Tell me the fucking number. I'm kind of in a hurry and busy."

"It's…"

Peyton sighed, not wanting to give away sensitive information right in front of Tricia. She might not be anything but a sweet girl he had met online, but Shay would kill him if she ever found out he gave out her flight number in front of a civilian.

"What's the fucking number, Peyton?"

"U102."

He nodded, satisfied with his answer. It'd be hard to know that referred to United 102 without context.

"Thanks." Shay's ragged breathing continued over the line for a moment.

*Just what I want to hear when I'm on a date.*

Tricia gave Peyton an awkward smile, confusion in her eyes. He lowered the phone just in time for the return of the waitress.

"Are you ready to order?"

Tricia nodded. "I'll have the pepperoni pizza."

"No pizza for me. Just a burger."

"Need you to see if you can ID someone for me," Shay murmured into the earpiece. "Need to make sure I don't have a tomb raider tail."

*Oh, this is going to be a long night.*

---

Tricia's stomach churned as Peyton opened the door to his apartment. She'd not gone home on a first date with a guy in a long time, but Peyton intrigued her. He seemed so nerdy, yet mysterious. Something about the combination was alluring, and it didn't hurt that the man was easy on the eyes.

She also would never, ever complain about her boss again. She might have to work weekends on occasion, but her boss would never call her four times in a single night to badger her about her job. There was no such thing as work-life balance at Peyton's start-up from what she could see.

Tricia stepped inside the sparsely decorated loft apartment with a smile. "I love how you're so close to the beach." She inhaled deeply. "You can even smell the ocean."

"Exactly." Peyton grinned.

A small orange tabby appeared from behind the couch and meowed at Tricia.

"What a pretty cat."

"That's Osiris." Peyton made an eager face and tilted his

head. "Ah, one sec. I have to go check on something." He hurried into his bedroom.

The woman almost laughed. He was cute, and she wouldn't mind having a little fun. He was probably checking if he had condoms.

Osiris meowed again, this time louder.

She knelt to pet the cat. She sighed at the same time. The cat rubbed against her hand and wandered off, no longer interested in humans.

The rather spartan decoration of the apartment gave the whole thing a very transitory vibe as if he'd not lived there long, but his profile claimed he'd been living in LA for a while.

She frowned as a faint lingering unease in the back of her mind shot to the front.

*How did I not notice before?*

Peyton was wearing some sort of earpiece. She'd been too embarrassed to ask him about it, thinking it was a hearing aid. She hadn't wanted to come off shallow, but she now realized that every time he'd spoken on his phone he didn't hold it up to his ear, but his mouth. The earpiece wasn't for a hearing aid at all.

What kind of man lived in a place that looked like he could abandon it with a day's notice and who needed to speak to his boss all the time? Two possibilities came to mind: spy or criminal.

Tricia swallowed. Peyton could be a serial killer. She grabbed her phone out of her purse and submitted the picture she'd taken when he was on the phone and his name to her Athena Shield Personal Protection App, now glad she had paid for the premium package. LA was full of weirdoes, after all.

She took a few deep breaths as she waited for the app to process his information and spit back public record entries. The app would at least help her confirm that he'd lived in LA for a while.

NO RECORDS FOUND.

Tricia blinked at the phone. She'd tried it on all her friends when she'd first downloaded it, and she'd never failed to find a record, even if it involved someone with the same name.

She adjusted a few settings and tried again.

NO RECORDS FOUND.

"Maybe there's something wrong with the app."

Tricia tapped her name and location as Los Angeles, but nothing else. She submitted the search.

Dozens of records links populated the screen within seconds.

The bedroom door opened and Peyton stepped out a broad smile on his face, his suit jacket already off.

"Do you want a drink?" he inquired.

Tricia shook her head. She nibbled on her lip and tried to calm her pounding heart. She stared down at her phone. It was like Peyton didn't even exist.

*Maybe he is a spy. But why would a spy be hooking up with women on dating sites? This could be some sort of trick to use me in some weird international intrigue thing.*

Tricia stopped herself from gasping. She worried about him being a spy or criminal, but he could be some sort of shape-changing Oriceran monster, too.

She headed over to the couch and dropped into it. "Why did you pick my profile?"

"Huh?"

"On Hello Cupid. Why me?"

Peyton smiled. "Because you're attractive and seemed a little quirky. In other words, my kind of girl."

"They don't have attractive and quirky girls at your company?"

He laughed and slid in beside her. She scooted to the other side of the couch.

"It's a very small company," Peyton explained. "Most start-ups are. The only woman who works at the place... Let's just say she's not my type."

"That your boss?"

A sheepish looked passed over his face. "Yeah. She's a real ball-buster."

"What's the company called?"

Peyton blinked as if the question had taken him off-guard. "Um, I'm under a non-disclosure agreement right now. I can't really talk about a lot of the details."

"You can't say the name of the company you're working for?" Tricia eyed him with suspicion.

Peyton shrugged. "That's the tech industry for you."

"Okay, sure, fine. What did you do before you worked for your super-secret company?"

"Freelance IT consulting." He waved a hand. "It's all very boring. You wouldn't be interested."

"But you lived in LA then?"

Peyton nodded. "Yeah."

"Here?"

"You mean this apartment?"

"Yeah."

"Um, no. This is kind of a newer place. Still kind of getting used to it."

Tricia narrowed her eyes. "Where did you live?"

"You sure you're not interested in a drink?" Peyton asked, a nervous tone in his voice. "I think I am. Do you mind?"

"Knock yourself out."

Peyton hopped up and headed into his kitchen.

Tricia reached into her purse and rested her hand on her pepper spray. Even shape-changing Oriceran monsters had eyes and mouths.

Peyton poured himself a glass of wine and gulped half of it down.

"Tell me more about your boss," Tricia pressed.

"My boss?" He gulped down the rest of the wine. "I can't...really talk about her much."

"Oh, come on. I've had friends who've signed NDAs. It's not like you're working for the CIA. You just can't talk about your day-to-day job." Her hand still in her purse, Tricia removed the cap of the pepper spray.

*Unless he is working for the CIA. I'm not going to be used for some weird spy games.*

Peyton walked back to the couch. "It's not like I can't talk about her. It's more that I don't want to. Does that make sense?"

Tricia stood, her gaze locked on Peyton. "Look, you seem nice, and you're cute, but I've got a headache, so I think I should head home."

"A headache?"

"Yeah."

Disappointment blasted over Peyton's face, and he sighed. "I'll drive you home."

She shook her head. "That's okay. I'm going to walk for a bit to clear my head and call a Lyft."

"You sure?" Peyton sighed again.

"Very sure." Tricia backed toward the door, her hand still on the pepper spray. "I hope you get a better job soon." Still facing Peyton, she opened the door and slipped through.

---

Peyton stared at the closed door for a good minute. The night had started awkwardly, but he'd thought Tricia agreeing to come back home with him was a good sign. He didn't understand what had brought on the game of Twenty Questions.

He dropped onto his couch face-first.

*It's never going to work, is it? I can't have a long-term relationship with the civilian population, and even a one-night stand seems like it'll be too much trouble.*

Peyton groaned and closed his eyes. It was hard being a dead guy.

Osiris hopped on the couch and rubbed against Peyton's face. At least his cat understood.

He opened his eyes. "Okay, if I can't have a real life separate from my work life, then no reason to keep you away from the warehouse." He nodded to himself. "You always were more of a warehouse cat. Lily misses you anyway."

S hay hummed as she pulled her Fiat into Warehouse Two, glad to be back in the US and away from any angry Greek or Turkish authorities. Dealing with the cops had given her more heartburn than the skeletons, which was not what she would have predicted when she took the job.

*What the fuck was that about? Most places I go the cops barely look at me, and suddenly in Turkey they were all over me? Did someone tip them off, or did they just get lucky?*

In the end, no one had managed to identify her, and she'd delivered the stone to the client. All in all, it had been a good solid job. She'd been paid, and her reputation continued to grow. She'd bounced back completely from her failure in Antarctica.

*Fuck Yulia. I hope she's trapped by a giant on some gnarly beanstalk now. She's gonna regret leaving me alive.*

Shay hopped out of her car and headed toward the office. The tomb raider was prepared to perch on the wall and practice her glare for the tardy Peyton, but to her pleasant surprise, he was already in the office tapping away at his computer with Lily by his side, learning something new. Like a Mad Magazine version of a family photo-op.

*This day is turning out great. I didn't even have to threaten him. Maybe it's not him, but an imposter who doesn't know him well enough to pretend to be late? Even Lily looks happy and involved.*

Shay snorted. The bright orange Nehru jacket dispelled any doubts she had about the man's identity. A small orange tabby sat on his lap. Somehow he'd gotten Lily involved in his new theme. She was wearing a white mini skirt and pink top.

"You look like Dr. Evil," Shay announced with a chuckle. "And his assistant?"

Peyton nodded. "That's what I was going for." Lily gave a nod.

"And that's fashionable?"

"It is to me."

She nodded toward the cat. "I didn't realize we needed a warehouse pet."

"That's what Lily's for." Peyton quickly held up the cat between himself and Lily, stroking the cat's fur. "Nice try." He looked up at Shay. "Is he going to be a problem?"

Shay shook her head. "Good thing about cats is that they can't give up your secret warehouse location in an interrogation since they can't talk."

"I guess I never really thought of it like that," he admitted. He continued to pet Osiris and cooed, "You going to tell the bad guys they can't break you?"

Shay laughed, imagining the cat speaking with Brownstone's deep voice for some reason. "Just make sure he stays inside."

"Easy enough," Peyton replied.

"Not like he's going to hack through all the security," said Lily. "That's even harder than speaking during an interrogation."

Shay chuckled. "Good point." Her gaze flicked to a big trash barrel she didn't remember being in the warehouse. She marched over to it. "What's this? You training for a new job with Purity Solutions?"

"Nope. It's a monument to self-improvement. A proof of how the flames of adversity have led to strength."

"What the hell does that mean?"

"You'll see."

Burnt remnants of what might once have been pizza lay inside. Judging by the volume, Peyton had made more than one attempt at pizza when she was gone, and somehow everything had gone very wrong, like some horrible pyromantic ritual that got out of hand.

Shay laughed. "Did a wizard raid the warehouse when I was out of the country? Looks like your brave pizzas sacrificed themselves to protect this place." She eyed the walls and ceiling. "But the question is, did they succeed? Did these pizzas die in vain, Peyton? Please tell me they didn't."

"Don't worry," he assured her. But behind his back Lily was busy nodding her head.

"I put the fire out before anyone noticed and called the fire department," continued Peyton. "No one even looked this way. I even checked security footage to verify that."

"What?" The humor vanished from Shay's voice. "The fire got that bad? How did you manage *that*?"

Peyton shrugged. "It wasn't a big deal. Lily helped me disable all the alarms before they could go off."

"And learned something about alarm systems," Lily chimed in.

Peyton held out his hand, smiling. "A learning opportunity for all involved. That's a good thing, right?"

Shay crossed her arms. "What useful tidbit did you learn from trying to burn down my warehouse? Where the fire extinguishers are?"

He grinned. "I learned that the sprinklers work."

The tomb raider shook her head. She couldn't take any more of this. If she wanted to salvage her mood, she'd need to get away from the warehouse right now.

Shay rolled her eyes. "Come on, we're going out for a celebratory breakfast."

"Come on, Osiris. Let's go get some human food."

Shay shook her head. "We're all going to a restaurant. Your cat can't come."

"Oh." Peyton made a pouty face.

---

Little Dom's was busy as usual. Every table both inside and out was occupied. Waitstaff flowed between the customers and tables like water, smiles on their faces. The customers seemed just happy, sipping their drinks and taking bites of their entrees.

Chatter filled the room and light music played in the background, but unlike many restaurants in the city, Shay could hear herself think.

She was never surprised when the place was a pleasant

madhouse. The restaurant had been famous as a pedestrian-friendly destination for longer than she'd been alive, which meant people were always popping in for a slice of Italian food heaven. It'd been a few weeks since she'd last been there, which was far too long.

Peyton thumbed through the menu. "What's good here?"

"Everything, but we're here to celebrate a successful job, so we're getting pizza." Shay gave him a serious look. "Tradition is important."

"Finally, decent pizza." Lily grabbed a menu, running her finger down the list.

Shay looked over at Peyton. "Tell me you didn't make her taste test."

Peyton eyed her quizzically, ignoring the question. "Pizza for breakfast?"

"Yep. They have breakfast pizza here. It's damned good."

"I'm surprised you tolerate breakfast pizza. Doesn't seem very New York-style purity or whatever."

Shay shrugged. "If someone's upfront about what they're doing I'm very tolerant. Little Dom's has two pizzas a person of taste can reasonably consume for breakfast." She held up a finger. "One is flatbread topped with smoked salmon, crescenza cheese, capers, and red onions." She held up a second finger. "Or, if you prefer, you can try the one with egg, speck, and mozzarella. Like I said, they are both damn good, and I've had them both several times."

"Okay, you've convinced me, and it doesn't sound like I have much of a choice."

"No, you don't."

"I think I'll have the second one. What about you two?"

Shay furrowed her brow. "I'm more in a salmon mood."

"Fish on a pizza? Yuck!"

Shay rolled her eyes. "What do you think anchovies are?"

"Well, I don't like them either."

"I've never had salmon. I'll try it," said Lily.

"You're both crazy."

"You need to expand your horizons, Peyton, especially if you want to become a true master of pizza and not just a wannabe."

Peyton snorted. "Says the woman who called Chicago-style pizza an abomination and a lot worse."

"Chicago has their own pizza? I have a lot left to learn." She glanced over at Shay. "No, not going to that boujee school."

Shay smirked. "Wasn't bringing that up. Hey, Peyton, there's expanding your horizons, and there's evil. I'm not a monster."

He chuckled.

They fell into silence until the waiter returned and they placed their orders.

The tomb raider waited until their server departed to speak again. "So, you tried to burn down the warehouse, poison Lily with your pizza, and you brought your cat to work. You're lucky I'm not allergic."

Peyton winced. He'd not even considered the possibility.

"Anything else happen while I was gone that I should know about? You join a boy band, too?"

"I'm okay at dancing but not that great at singing."

Peyton shook his head. "And nothing much, really. I've been trying to look into those symbols for you using a lot of heavy-duty image-matching algorithms, but I haven't found anything yet."

"Not a big deal." Shay nodded slowly. She'd held back before because she wanted to see if he stumbled onto anything without being led there. But she decided it wouldn't hurt to nudge him onto the right track.

She leaned forward and lowered her voice. "Poke around people interested in underworld alien shit. See what you can turn up for the symbols in that context."

"Aliens? As in extraterrestrials, Oricerans, or visiting Mexican citizens?" asked Lily with a mouth full of pizza. "Whoa."

"The first. Just see where that leads you."

The researcher nodded, a hint of excitement in his eyes. "You found something pointing that way? You really think it's that and not just people misinterpreting Oriceran stuff?"

"Maybe. Hard to say. Doesn't hurt for you to check into it." Shay picked up her coffee and took a sip. "Twenty years ago, most people were skeptical about magic being real. When the world is insane, insane explanations make a lot more sense." She shrugged, setting down her coffee. "I find magic items for a living, and I've run into a lot of weird shit."

"If this involves aliens, are you saying it was an alien demon you fought?" Peyton rubbed his temples. "That kind of hurts to think about."

"I don't know, could be. Or it could be nothing more

than a crazy elf with delusions of grandeur. My...solution to the issue seemed to handle him okay."

Peyton laughed. "You know, both of our lives used to be a lot simpler and safer. I never used to worry about things like demons, alien or otherwise."

"Shit happens, then you die." Shay shrugged. "And if you're really lucky, you don't come back as a skeleton or zombie."

"Amen," said Lily.

A man in a long trench coat bumped into a woman outside. Shay couldn't make out what he was saying, but it seemed like he was apologizing. If she'd not been watching closely, she might have missed his hand sliding into the woman's purse.

If Little Dom's hadn't been one of her favorite places Shay might have been impressed by the man's pickpocketing skill, but his presence ruined what should have been an otherwise relaxing post-job victory meal.

"I have some ideas on how to improve some of our notification systems," Peyton began. "Okay, Lily and I have some ideas. Also, if you take more time between jobs, I'll have more time to improve things instead of having to concentrate on support and always playing catch-up."

Shay gave him a distracted nod as she watched the pickpocket take another man's wallet. She shot up. "You know what the problem with our world is?"

"Where did that come from? I was talking about notification systems and improving our IT resources. Is the problem with our world outdated electronic notification infrastructure?"

Lily gave him a nudge and nodded toward the door. She

had noticed the same thing and kept looking back and forth between the pickpocket and the tomb raider, learning.

Shay locked her attention on the pickpocket as he entered the restaurant and made his way toward the bar. He nicked the wallet of a man at the bar while reaching over him with his other hand for a straw.

"The problem is that too many people don't quit while they're ahead," Shay explained.

"Some people might say that about you."

Shay snorted. "They're probably right." She grabbed her cup. "I'll be right back. I'm going to get a refill."

"You can't wait?"

Lily shook her head, rolling her eyes. "How are you so good at what you do and so clueless about so many other things?"

"No. I can't. This stuff isn't Turkish coffee," said Shay. "It doesn't have the same punch to keep me going."

Shay marched to the bar and looked the opposite way. She bumped into the pickpocket.

The man grunted.

Shay let out a feigned embarrassed giggle and lowered her free hand inside his jacket.

"Sorry about that," she offered. "I don't even have an excuse unless I'm still drunk from last night. I should watch where I'm going."

"No problem." The pickpocket shrugged. "I wasn't paying much attention myself."

"You sure you're okay? I could pay for your food or something if I ruined your morning. My therapist says I need to be spreading goodwill in the world, and I'd just be *so* hurt if I'd started a man's day off on the wrong foot."

He shook his head. "No. I'm fine. Seriously. No big deal. If that's the worst thing that happens to me today, I'll be pretty happy."

Shay managed to slide the bar patron's wallet out of the pickpocket's jacket and stepped back. She tossed it behind the victim's stool.

The pickpocket looked behind him and frowned.

"What's that?" Shay stepped over to the stool and picked up the wallet. She handed it to the bar patron. "I think you dropped this, sir."

The man at the bar took the wallet, his eyes wide. "Huh. Thanks. It's good to know there are still people in this city looking out for each other."

"No problem." Shay spun back to the pickpocket and focused a cold stare on him. "I mean, losing your wallet at breakfast might ruin a person's whole day, and I know what my therapist would say about that." She let the feigned ditziness fade from her voice and the natural hard edge return.

The criminal swallowed and bolted toward the door. Shay was half-tempted to go after him and take him down, but she didn't need police showing up and poking around her background. He barreled into a man on the way out.

"Hey, watch it, bro." The man shoved the criminal.

The criminal didn't even slow. He ran around the man and threw open the doors to complete his escape.

Shay sauntered back to her table, snickering. "What were you saying about the notifications, Peyton?"

The researcher blinked several times and shook his

head. "What the hell just happened? I saw it, but I don't understand it. I thought you were getting coffee." He pointed to her cup. "But you didn't refill it."

"I didn't want a pickpocket thinking he could mess with one of my restaurants. It makes for a bad atmosphere. I made it clear he needed to leave."

"Oh. I thought we were just going out for breakfast, not breakfast and a show."

Shay shrugged. "I try to keep it interesting."

"I'll say." The man chuckled. "Anyway, it's just about better networking the computer systems to improve the notifications. I'm filtering a lot of them, but I want to set up a database so I can put categories on them and you can review them more easily. That way you don't have to waste as much time sorting through the information. Or is that a stupid idea?"

"No, it's not. It's a good idea." Shay shrugged. "You've been working with me long enough now that you know what I need. Check with me before you implement, but if you have a good idea toss it to me and I'll let you know."

Peyton might need to be kept in line every now and again, but it was stupid to pretend he wasn't integral to her tomb raider operation. Anything he could do to cut down on the amount of bullshit she had to sort through would only improve her efficiency.

The man had become a useful part of her team, not just a tool or an investment. Even Lily was starting to grow on her as a part of their team.

Shay nodded. It was time. "Remember when I mentioned showing you a new warehouse?"

Peyton nodded. "Yeah. I just figured you'd get around to it when you were ready."

"Wrong angle. It's more about when *you* were ready."

"I think I am."

Shay chuckled. "Of course you'd *say* that."

"Well, how do I prove I'm ready?"

"You already have. Let's eat breakfast and go check it out."

"Does any of this include me?" asked Lily.

"You're the fave child. I thought that went without saying," said Peyton.

# 21

"Talk about anticlimactic," Peyton grumbled. He shook his head and gestured at the racks and shelves of equipment. "Did you hit your head in Turkey? I come to Warehouse Three all the time. I figured out where this place was without you even telling me, remember? I've even shown this to Lily while you were out of town. Don't reach for your gun. You okayed it, remember?"

Shay smirked. Sometimes it felt nice to take an arrogant person down a peg or two.

"Sure, but do you know about the Annex?"

Peyton blinked. "What Annex?"

Shay laughed. "I'm kind of surprised you haven't figured it out already. There's an entire other building connected to this one."

Shay noticed Lily smile. She had already found it. Damn, maybe that girl would surpass her faster than she thought. And smart enough to keep it to herself. No way she gained entry.

"What? That? I've looked through the surveillance

footage. It's just empty space. That's your big secret? I figured you just kept the space because it's already connected to the building and you can't risk renting it out."

"Follow me." Shay walked toward a spot of wall near the corner. "Come and be amazed by what I can still pull over on you."

"What a wonderful wall you've discovered. It's so… wall-like and gray."

Shay winked. "Sometimes, the best place to hide something is in plain sight, you know."

"Which is why you forced me to live hidden in a warehouse for so long."

"*Sometimes* it's the best place. It's not *always* the best place."

She placed her palm in the middle of the wall and hissed at the faint burning sensation of the hidden DNA reader. A small panel opened to reveal a retinal scanner and a keypad. She leaned forward as it scanned her eye and she entered the code.

Loud grinding filled the room as the wall slid open to reveal a hallway.

Peyton blinked several times. "What the hell? What about the door in the lobby?"

"If you had opened it, you would have found it's been filled with cement. I really expected you to try, you know."

Peyton sighed. "I just figured that with the surveillance footage there wasn't a point. I never figured you'd try so hard to trick me. Besides, Lily might rat me out to get back at me."

"That's not the way retribution works," said Lily, peering into the hallway.

"You already found this hallway, didn't you." Shay watched Lily try to feign surprise. Okay, lying was not a strength. Good thing to know.

"What? You knew and didn't tell me? I thought we had a pact?" Peyton asked, anguished.

"This seemed beyond the scope of our pact."

"How did you get in there?"

"Weird magic, I told you. Comes in handy at the oddest times."

"You're going to have to show me some time," said Shay.

"We'll make a trade," said Lily.

"My tricks had nothing to do with you, Peyton. I set up all this before I ever thought of saving your skinny ass."

"But why didn't you tell me about it earlier?"

Shay shrugged. "It was a test, especially after your little stunts earlier tracking down warehouses, I was curious to see if you could find out about it yourself. The surveillance footage is bullshit, obviously."

Peyton shook his head. "I can't believe this has been here the entire time and I didn't even know about it. I'm both embarrassed and impressed."

"I still have a few secrets, Peyton. Don't underestimate me just because you've managed to get a few over on me."

He laughed. "I respect and fear you, but I never underestimate you."

"I just respect you," said Lily.

Shay gestured to the hallway and entered. Buzzing lights clicked on with each step she took.

Peyton hurried after her. "Why do I half-suspect I'll find Narnia at the other end?"

"What's Narnia?" asked Lily. "Don't mention the school again, just help me out."

"I have a book for you later. And Peyton, I had some Turkish Delight when I was in Turkey. I wasn't that impressed."

"What kind of candy would you sell your family out for?"

Shay snickered. "We both have shitty families. It's not like we need candy to sell them out."

They reached the end of the hallway where another set of DNA and retinal scanners, along with a keypad, awaited.

After the requisite security ritual the door slid open and bright lights flooded the space, revealing row after row of wigs, clothing, and accessories. Dozens of cars filled half the room, ranging from a rusty station wagon to a bright yellow Lamborghini.

Shay pointed to an elevator across the room. "There's a second floor, too. No cars up there, though."

"Can I have a car?" Lily stood there with her mouth half open.

"You're not even old enough to drive."

"Hasn't stopped me yet."

"The Warehouse Three Annex is your closet and garage all in one?" Peyton surveyed the warehouse, awestruck.

"That's one way to look at it." Shay pointed to a computer in a small office near the hall. "Have a database in there with a catalog of everything. It's all carefully arranged—the clothing or cars needed for any identity. Not only do I have the individual pieces stored, but each car has the stuff needed for a couple weeks in a given identity. Documents, account numbers—that sort of thing."

Peyton shook his head. "Why do you even have all this?"

"I used to have a warehouse like this in New York for my old job."

"I get why you needed that. It's not like you announced who you were when you killed people."

Shay shook her head. "You, more than anyone else, know how everything we do leaves a trace somewhere. If you're not actively trying to avoid it, you'll end up with a trail that leads back to you."

"But you never got caught. You faked your death."

"Yeah, and that worked because of how careful I was. Don't you get it? As far as the cops know, Shay Carson never killed anyone. Some other person did. In fact, *different* people did, and this is how I maintained that. Different appearances, documents, identities, cars. Whatever I needed." She started walking down one of the rows. "There are two ways to handle trails. One way is to try not to leave one. The second is to leave a false trail. Or ten false trails."

Peyton wandered after her and whistled. "This is like gangster's Halloween." He put on an impressive velvet broad-brimmed hat with a feather. "I think I'd take on jobs all the time just to try out the different outfits."

Lily slid on oversized Jackie-O style sunglasses and a large floppy hat.

Shay chuckled. "It's not for fun. I don't wear or use any of this shit unless it's for the fake identity. If I have any reason to think an identity's been compromised I burn it."

"How do you burn an identity?"

"Same way as before. I destroy everything associated with it."

Peyton swallowed. "Everything?"

"Don't worry, I'm not gonna kill you anytime soon."

"I'm not worried about me." He pointed to the Lamborghini. "I'm worried about that beautiful thing. You wouldn't destroy the car."

"I got rid of more than a few sports cars during my years as a killer." Shay let the word slip out before she knew it and quickly looked at Lily.

Lily took off the hat and moved on to a rack of dresses.

"I already told her about your old profession. It was less of a big reveal than you would imagine." Peyton groaned. "How many cars? That's just…wrong."

She almost laughed at the idea of him being more offended by her destruction of sports cars than her murdering people. They were a regular Addams Family. "Cars can always be replaced. They're just things, in the end."

"In that case, maybe I should take it for a spin. Just in case you need to destroy it later. I'd like to have the experience." He nodded toward the Lamborghini. "You might not even have a reason to drive any of these."

"I call shotgun!" yelled Lily.

"You can't drive the Lamborghini."

Peyton threw up his hands. "What about the Aston Martin, then?"

"Nope. Not that one either."

"What about the—"

Shay cut him off with a glare. "No cars. These are part of identities, and you don't have the tits to pull off most of them."

"Just asking." Peyton set down the velvet hat and picked

up a beret. "Look at me, I'm a revolutionary leader. Down with the bourgeoisie!"

Shay chuckled, and Lily put on a top hat and spun him around.

They both all but skipped down the rows, looking at hats and jackets. "I could put together some awesome outfits." He pulled down an old Army jacket. "I didn't think about it until just now, but you have both men and women's clothing here."

"Sometimes it helps to play up my feminine wiles, and sometimes it helps for people to not even notice you." She nodded toward the station wagon. "That one's attached to a man's identity."

"A cross-dressing Shay? It's hard to imagine."

"I did it when I needed to." She shrugged. "It was all about getting close to the target. I did what I had to do to kill them. Depending on the country and location, being a woman might not get me close enough."

"And now?" asked Lily, twirling around with a sparkling black dress held in front of her.

"Now I'm a tomb raider. It's less about fake identities, but we both know shit can turn on a dime. This crap with Yulia reminded me that I'm gonna rack up a few enemies in this new career and I need to take that into account. I might need a disguise or fake identity for future jobs." Shay gestured around the warehouse. "All of this may be necessary on some of my jobs, so it's best if you become familiar with what's in here. That way you can provide proper support."

Peyton gave a solemn nod. "I think to become truly

familiar with everything I'll need to test drive the cars. With my colleague, of course."

Shay smirked and pointed to the station wagon. "Like I said, that one's attached to a man's identity. You can drive it."

"Huh. Not so interested in that."

"Okay, I've got to get going." Shay pulled out her phone and tapped on her custom security app. "Both of your biometrics should now work with the Annex's doors." She spun on her heel and waved. "And put back all that crap where you found it before you leave."

"But…" Peyton groaned.

---

A few hours later, Shay relaxed at Warehouse Two with a book on the purported influence of aliens on history: *From Vimanas to Ezekiel's Wheel.*

The book wasn't from Warehouse Four, but instead had been borrowed from a local library. It had been published in the early 2000s. One problem with more modern books on the subject was that they all assumed every mysterious piece of history could be explained away by Oriceran contact.

A century of speculation about aliens had been tossed away and was now considered a worse explanation than the influence of creatures like elves, Atlanteans, and gnomes.

Shay snickered at the thought.

Having the truth about Oriceran come out might have cracked the old dogma, but the new paradigm was just as narrow-minded. The level of decent knowledge on the issue was pretty damned low, unfortunately. Sometimes, though, the crazies had been right all along.

Peyton tapped at his keyboard in the office. Lily was back between the cubicles, taking a nap.

Peyton sped up, the keys clacking. A few seconds later he increased his speed even more, his pace now furious.

Shay set her book down and glanced at him. "What did that keyboard ever do to you? Does it owe you money?"

He shot up, pushing his chair out of the way. Osiris leapt to the ground, hissing.

"No, no, no." Peyton ran his hands through his hair. "This is bad. Very bad."

Shay rushed into the office. "Talk to me."

Peyton took a deep breath. "It's Randy."

"Okay, you need to clue me in, here. You're freaking out, and I don't know what the hell is going on."

"I found some people poking around—digging. It's not random. It's obvious they suspect I'm still alive and are looking for evidence. I've traced them to my brother."

Shay sighed and nodded. "That might not mean anything. He might just be nervous and double-checking. Being thorough is a good move, but you've covered your tracks well."

"Or maybe you were right, and he saw me when I went to my father's grave."

"Not a chance." Shay shook her head.

Peyton eyed her. "*Not a chance?* You were the one who made it sound like it was a dumb move. You bitched a lot about it at the time."

"It *was* a dumb move, but that doesn't change the fact

that I made sure that no one saw us." She nodded to the computer. "You know what to do. You saying these losers he's hired are better than you?"

"No," Peyton grumped.

"Hell, you've already traced them to your brother. That shows how sloppy they are."

He nodded once. "Yeah, you're right. These guys are damned sloppy. Randy should have offered more money to get some better guys."

Shay snorted. "Then fucking clamp down on all their attempts, but make it clear it's not you. If they don't track you down, it doesn't matter if your brother is sniffing around."

The hacker nodded and sat back down, his face a mask of grim determination. "You're right. I can do this. I'll show these assholes who the real computer expert is." He frowned. "I'm going to be the ghost haunting them, but they'll never even see me."

Shay stepped out of the office, her thoughts still swirling. They needed a more permanent solution to deal with Randy. Peyton wouldn't be able to reclaim any sort of actual life if his brother was waiting to kill him the first time he popped his head up.

She glanced over her shoulder at her assistant.

*We'll see where this goes, Peyton. Sometimes, though, it comes down to kill or be killed. Are you ready for that?*

---

Shay hummed to herself as she opened the door to her home. She chuckled, remembering Peyton mentioning needing his own place so he could bring women there. She wondered how the man intended to meet women when he had to keep such a low profile.

*What's the guy going to do? Lie to his girlfriend constantly?*

She laughed at the absurdity of it all. Until they took care of his brother, one way or another, he'd need to get used to being alone.

Her phone rang, breaking her out of the thoughts, and she pulled it out of her purse. She'd expected it to be the bounty hunter but was surprised by a different, albeit familiar, number.

"Hey, Professor. Didn't expect a call from you at this time of night."

"Good evening, Miz Carson. I never know when you're going to be available, so I figured it's always best to call as soon as I'm interested.

"That's a good policy."

The Professor chuckled. "Ah, right then. I called to tell you I'd like to meet with you tomorrow evening to discuss another job opportunity, one that is time-sensitive."

"Is it the one you were talking about before?"

"Aye. I've finally gathered all the details I need, and I'd like to get on it sooner rather than later. We potentially have a narrow window."

"Nothing new about that," Shay observed. "I'm assuming you want me to meet you at the same place?"

"Aye. I feel most comfortable at the pub." The Professor laughed.

Curiosity bubbled up. "Why?"

"Why what?"

"Why do you feel so comfortable at some Irish pub discussing serious business instead of some locked-down office or something somewhere?

"I can see how that might confuse a person." The Professor exhaled loudly. "Do you know the legend of the Leanan Sídhe?"

"Your bar has a legend? I imagine it involves some old tomb raider who once drank from a magical infinite beer glass but managed to empty it. Or that Bard of Filth thing."

The Professor laughed. "The first would be truly a wondrous thing, and the second is grand, but no, I was speaking of the eponymous faerie."

"Don't know a lot about Leanan Sídhe. They are Celtic faeries. They take a lover and drain their lifeforce, but it's not totally a parasitic thing because they can act as a muse and provide inspiration to artists. Their lovers will die young, but their work will leave a great impact." She blew out a breath. "I don't know if they are real. I've run into too many legendary creatures to assume they aren't."

"Aye, that about covers it. There are variations to the legends, but you mentioned all the most important points."

Shay furrowed her brow. "Why are we suddenly having a quiz on Celtic faeries? Does the job involve one, or do you just really like the name of the bar?"

"I do like the name, but it goes deeper than that." The Professor chuckled. "Because I'm going to grant you a gift, rare insight into my background. I like the place because, first and foremost, the beer is of excellent quality, and secondly, because the name is a reminder that greatness often has a cost. Few people accomplish anything of merit without sacrifice."

Shay shrugged. "True enough, but some people don't seek greatness."

"Alas, sometimes greatness is thrust upon people."

"Not if people are hiding well enough."

The Professor chuckled. "I suppose. We'll talk again tomorrow, Miz Carson." He ended the call before she could reply.

Shay stared at the phone.

*I think I like happy Father O'Banion more than the brooding, philosophical Professor.*

---

Shay wondered which of Smite-Williams' faces she was going to have to deal with as she pushed into the pub and made her way through the crowd to the Professor's preferred booth in the back. He gave her a slight wave and took a sip of his beer as she sat across from him.

"Good evening, Miz Carson."

His cheeks weren't all that red, which was a good sign. Or maybe it wasn't. It was hard to be sure about the man.

Not only that, she assumed Smite-Williams used his drunken reputation and persona to manipulate people's perceptions of him when it suited his needs. The man reeked of competence and danger in a way even Brownstone didn't.

Shay nodded. "What do you have for me, Professor?"

"A simple job."

"Simple jobs don't require tomb raiders, especially ones who want as much money as I do."

The Professor laughed. "It's simple in that no one else is looking for the artifact and it's not being defended. It's just in a difficult and dangerous location to access."

Shay nodded. "'Simpler,' then. Not 'simple.'"

"Aye." The Professor downed some more beer before continuing. "There are subterranean caves connected to Lake Michigan near Chicago. Normally, the caves aren't accessible except under certain conditions. I've become aware that the caves are currently passable and will be for a short period, which is why I spoke of this job being time-sensitive."

Shay narrowed her eyes. "What conditions? I need to know what I'm getting into."

"Cold, mostly. It interfaces with a magical spell that normally both blocks and cloaks the caves. Even when they are exposed, the spell keeps the water out."

*Cold? Yulia better not show up. Actually, no, I hope she does so I can show her who is more dangerous.*

"Neat trick. So, you want me to swim into some caves from Lake Michigan? Sounds like fun."

"Aye. These caves will be flooded, so you'll need to be extra careful."

Shay chuckled. "Pretty damn cold in Lake Michigan right now."

"Says the woman who dove into a lake in the Alps." He punctuated his sentence with a sip of his beer. "I'm sure it won't prove much of a problem for a woman of your experience and talents."

"Not saying it will be, but also not saying I love swimming in cold water, even geared up."

"Understandable," the Professor replied.

Shay wasn't that worried about the water, all bitching aside. She was more concerned about her target.

"What's in the caves?"

"A small stone with symbols on it. Very small. Very portable, unlike large ancient Chinese weapons." The Professor set down his beer and pulled out his phone. "You might find something else there, but this job—and the money—is focused on this stone. That's what I'm paying you to find."

Shay's face twitched. A black and white photo of a familiar-looking stone filled the screen. The shape was slightly different than the one she'd recovered from Mexico, but at least some of the symbols were identical.

She should know. She'd spent more than a few hours staring at the stone from Mexico.

"What is this?" Shay inquired, trying to keep her

burning curiosity out of her voice. Having an information advantage over Smite-Williams was rare.

"You don't need to know, Miz Carson. You just need to recover the artifact. I'll send you information on the likely location when you agree to take the job."

"Bullshit," Shay hissed.

The Professor blinked, taken off guard by her sudden vehemence. "Excuse me?"

"I need to know about the stone," Shay insisted.

"I'm surprised by your reaction. I can assure you that in its current form the artifact is not dangerous at all, if that's what you're worried about. I don't understand your concern otherwise."

"I need to know what's going on with this one," Shay demanded. "I have my reasons."

"No, Miz Carson, I don't think you need to know more than what I'm offering." The Professor pushed his beer to the side. "I understand you need all relevant information, but I can guarantee you there won't be any problems or tricks if you recover this stone. It won't explode. You won't have to keep it in any sort of special container or use dampening magic. You just have to swim into the lake, enter the caves, find the artifact, and bring it to me. It's just a stone with symbols as far as this job is concerned."

"Let's cut the crap." Shay leaned forward and shook her head. "They're not just symbols. They are symbols that might be extraterrestrial in origin, and I'm not talking about Oriceran. Everything we thought we knew once the truth of Oriceran came out might be just as wrong as what people believed twenty years ago."

The tomb raider couldn't remember if she'd ever seen

true surprise from Smite-Williams. The man stared at her wide-eyed for several seconds before gulping down the rest of his beer.

"While not admitting anything else," the Professor began, "I'll note that you are surprisingly well-informed about this particular stone. I didn't anticipate this scenario."

Shay sighed. "I came across some information related to these symbols. I've looked into it as deeply as I can, and everything I can find points to it being from some other planet, not Earth or Oriceran." She shook her head. "I don't know how to read the symbols yet, but some of them match. There's no fucking way this other stone isn't related to it."

"I see." The Professor scratched his eyebrow. "That revelation changes a few things."

"Does it now?"

"Aye. I have to contact a few people."

Shay frowned. "So, I'm off the job."

"I didn't say that. If anything, your knowledge makes you the superior choice for this. I'll get back to you soon."

Shay chuckled. "I just realized something. You didn't know, did you?"

The Professor shot her a smile. "As I said, I'll get back to you, but I'd ask that you stay in town, so I can get a hold of you."

"Just don't take too long."

"Oh, trust me, I'm not planning to."

## 23

P eyton whistled while Osiris slept on his lap. Lily was up but rooting around in the refrigerator. His panic over his brother had subsided. Now he wasn't afraid. He was filled with contempt.

Shay was right. Peyton was far better than whatever lame mercenary hackers Randy had hired. It was almost too easy to redirect their searches and cover his tracks.

The key strategy to hacking was not to be discovered. That way you could take your time manipulating the target system. If they'd been halfway decent he wouldn't have even known they were looking for him, and now they didn't have a chance.

With all that taken care of, Peyton had more time to look into Shay's allegedly alien symbols. He clicked his mouse on a window to inspect the results from his custom dark web bots. He doubted just searching the surface net was going to reveal anything Shay didn't already know.

For all her bristly killer persona he'd seen some of the

woman underneath, the history-obsessed tomb raider with a vast library. Peyton was good at research, but Shay was damned good too.

His bots had been crawling around the web seeking out information that might be of help, but he'd barely had time to look at their results. The best computer program in the world was still useless without some human curation in the end.

If there really were aliens who had nothing to do with Oriceran, it only followed that people might have spent as much time trying to cover up the truth of their existence as they had magic. Access to advanced alien technology and magic would be the perfect tools for conspirators.

The only reason Peyton had hope was that people—whether from Oriceran or Earth—tended to make some small mistake in the end. It was one of the reasons hackers still relied heavily on tricking people out of information before they even worried about getting behind a keyboard.

"What do we have here? Something good?" Peyton murmured to himself.

He scanned the search results from the bots. Their algorithms focused on locating dark web pages related to non-Oriceran alien languages and linguistics, with exclusions for certain famous fictional alien languages. Most of the hits were garbage from troll sites or raving conspiracy nuts, but one result caught his eye.

**PROJECT NEPHILIM SUMMARY AND BUDGETARY ALLOTMENTS.**

Peyton chewed on his lip. "Yeah, that doesn't sound ominous. Let's see where you're coming from, Project Nephilim."

He typed in a few commands. "Department of Defense server, huh? Why am I not surprised? Of course it is."

Peyton worked his jaw for a moment. Poking around in a DOD server might bring some heat...but only if he got caught. The spider had already port-scanned for him. For a military server, they had a lot of holes.

*I should write my congressman to complain about this sad display.*

He spent the next few minutes digging into the Project Nephilim server while making sure to cover his tracks and maintain a healthy number of proxy servers between the DOD and his computer.

*Yeah, I bet Randy's hired guns couldn't accomplish that on their best day.*

"Let's see how you're wasting our taxpayer dollars."

Peyton downloaded every document he could get his hands on. He could browse them at his leisure later.

"I'm too damn good at this. It's almost not fair."

Osiris meowed in response.

"Yeah, glad you agree."

---

After twenty minutes, an alarm chimed on his computer.

"Shit, what now? Randy's boys coming back at me?"

Nope. It was someone at the DOD. Someone was back-tracking his connection through his proxy servers, but it would be another fifteen minutes before he had all the files.

"Okay, so they have a few good IT guys after all. Come on, download faster, damn it."

Lily walked up behind him, a spoon dangling from her mouth and the last of the ice cream in her hands. "What's happening?"

"Shit's breaking out all over."

Several more proxy servers fell to the trace despite Peyton's redirection, but he still needed twelve minutes. The counter-hacker was closing on him far too swiftly.

"Faster, faster, faster. I can do this."

Peyton terminated all other running CPU processes except the downloads and killed all other bandwidth usage in the warehouse network.

The trace had made it through eighty percent of his proxy servers with ten minutes still required.

Peyton gritted his teeth. "Fuck you, DOD White Hat. You didn't win. I still got a bunch of files, and you didn't identify me." He terminated the connection with only two proxy servers between him and detection.

Lily leaned over and studied the screen. "That was close, wasn't it?"

"Too close. Now let's see what we got. I hope it's something good and not a bunch of boring spreadsheets."

---

"Shay, you need to see this right now," Peyton yelled from the office.

The tomb raider grumbled, "This better not be some slasher movie that's emotionally scared you. If you don't want to see it, stay on the safe sites."

Peyton sighed. "It's nothing like that. I pulled a bunch of

files off a DOD server when I was looking into your symbols. I couldn't get them all without being caught, but I still managed a good haul."

"Okay, now you've got my attention. Find anything interesting?"

"He's been very busy," nodded Lily.

Peyton nodded and grinned, then stood and motioned to the chair. "I just spent a couple of hours going through the world's most boring encoded budget spreadsheets." He made a face. "The government sure loves their budgets."

"That doesn't sound interesting, so why I am here?"

"Yeah, but then I found a summary document for the project all the budget crap's related to." He pointed to the screen. "Check this out."

The tomb raider sat and started reading aloud. "Existing human- and machine-intelligence-based translation resources are insufficient to translate the ideographs identified on the stone. Extensive investigation and cross-referencing have confirmed that the symbols have no links to any extant or extinct Earth-based writing system, either ideographic or phonographic in nature."

An image of a stone appeared beneath the first few sentences. The shape looked different than the stone in Mexico or Michigan, but many of the symbols matched.

"That's three of them," she murmured to herself.

"Three stones?" Lily asked.

"Yep. This one, the one I found, and one the Professor wants me to find."

"Oh," said Peyton.

Shay continued reading. "Our consultations with

Oriceran experts confirm the symbols have no links to any extant or extinct Oriceran-based writing system, either purely representational or related to extra-dimensional or so-called magical processes." Shay blinked and looked up. "Holy shit."

Peyton bobbed his head. "Keep reading. It gets better."

"Spectrographic inspection of the relevant recovered artifacts confirms isotopic content that is not consistent with a terrestrial origin. Metallurgical and magical analysis lends further support to a non-terrestrial origin.

"In coordination with the findings of PROJECT HOUDINI, our recommendation is to apply additional resources to the translation and decoding of the symbols. Without better knowledge of the semantics of the symbols, we are unable at this time to establish if this likely-extraterrestrial writing is linked to a civilization or group of civilizations that may present a possible threat to the safety of Earth and the territorial integrity and safety of the United States."

Shay shook her head and looked up at Peyton. "That's pretty heavy-duty stuff."

Peyton bounced on his toes a few times. "That's the government basically admitting they have alien writing and don't have a damned clue what it means."

"Sounds like it, but what's Project Houdini?"

The researcher shrugged. "No clue. I can't find a reference to it in any of the other documents. I haven't checked online. Whatever it is, it's locked down pretty tight. I think I got really lucky on this one. Some guy just left a few ports open when they shouldn't have."

Shay rubbed her chin. "At a minimum, this shit proves I'm not crazy. That stone is alien."

"This is weird magic, even for me," said Lily.

Peyton sighed. "Damn it."

"What's wrong? This is a good catch! You did a great job."

He shook his head. "But it also proves the government can't translate it, and they might be throwing millions of dollars at it. What hope do we have?"

"Don't know. We'll have to wait and see. I'm thinking we're gonna have to find out more about this shit sooner rather than later." She laughed. "Guess you stumbled onto something big by spotting that shit about the missing tomb raider."

Peyton looked stunned. "I did, didn't I? I don't know how I feel about that."

"Way to go, Peyton." Lily patted him on the back.

They really are getting to be like family, thought Shay.

Her phone rang.

"Speak of the Devil," she murmured.

Peyton looked confused. "Huh? Is it the dead tomb raider?"

"Nope." Shay held up a hand. "What's up, Professor?"

"You need to come to the pub," he replied.

"Sure, I can meet you tomorrow."

"No. Now."

Shay blinked. "What?"

Smite-Williams took a deep breath before continuing, "You need to come right now. It's about the job. Make sure you come alone. If you don't come tonight, I'll be forced to make other arrangements."

Shay pushed into the pub and marched straight toward the Professor's booth, a frown on her face. She didn't like being ordered around, but at the same time, she had no doubt that his call had something to do with the alien language she was investigating.

Given how spooked he seemed, she didn't think it wise to question it too much.

She stopped a few yards from the table. The Professor had told her to come alone, but *he* wasn't alone. A tall silver-haired Light Elf sat beside Smite-Williams with a weary expression on his face.

"Should I come back?" Shay inquired, keeping her attention on the elf.

The Professor nodded to a seat. "Correk has an interest in the object I want you to recover, so I asked him to come to this meeting."

"And who is Correk, exactly—other than an elf?"

"You don't need that information at this time."

Shay sighed and rolled her eyes. "You know what? In the spirit of being a good example of sharing, and proving I'm on the ball here, I'm gonna give you some more information, even though you're being...difficult."

The Professor nodded. "And what information are you going to give me, Miz Carson?"

"The government has one of the stones. They know it's extraterrestrial, but they can't translate it. They've consulted Oriceran experts and human experts."

An uncomfortable look spread over Correk's face, and the elf cleared his throat. "I'm curious about something."

Shay stared at him. "And what's that?"

"How did you know about all of this to begin with?" The elf nodded at the Professor. "He mentioned you'd already been investigating this before he offered you the job."

Shay shot Correk a grin. "I'm very resourceful, and I'm interested in ancient history. This is a big deal. Hell, it's as big a deal as the truth about Oriceran coming out. Another planet with intelligent beings, and they've visited us in the past."

Correk let out a quiet sigh. "It is at that."

The tomb raider narrowed her eyes. "You're not interested in it for the language or history, though, are you?"

The elf shook his head. "No."

"Then why are you interested in it?"

"I have my reasons."

"And they are?"

"You don't need to know."

Shay's gaze ticked over to the Professor. "You have a Light Elf here. That makes me think it's not just some stone with writing. It's obviously got some magical power."

She wasn't ready to reveal she had a stone. The Professor and Correk were less than forthcoming, so the tomb raider didn't see any advantage in being any more helpful than she'd already been.

The Professor sighed. "I can assure you, Miz Carson, the only danger you'll face from that stone is in the process of recovering it." The Professor and Correk shared a glance. "And I'm willing to double your fee for its recovery."

"Huh. Well, when you put it that way, how can I refuse?"

The Professor smiled and picked up his previously-neglected glass of beer. "Now that's what I wanted to hear."

# 24

Shay surveyed the gathered gear on several tables in Warehouse Three. Pistols, grenades, underwater flares, amphibious needle guns, more than a few jammers, both aerial and aquatic drones, and of course, her cold-weather diving gear. It was almost everything she'd need for a raid where she wasn't expecting a fight.

*Then again, I wasn't expecting a fight in Antarctica either.*

"You two did a good job of getting my equipment ready. A damned good job."

Peyton smiled. "Lily did a lot of the smaller arms. You don't need a disguise or fake identity this time?" His gaze drifted longingly to the wall concealing the entrance to the Annex. "I'm sure we could find something in there that will work."

"Nope. This is a straightforward raid, and if I do it right I won't even be dealing with anyone other than to drop off my rental car and get on the plane. I'm only hoping I don't get in a firefight under the lake."

Lily patted the long black needle gun. "This baby has plenty of ammo."

"You have to understand, fighting underwater always sucks."

"Why? As long as you have the right weapon it's not a big deal, right?" asked Peyton.

Shay shook her head. "Fighting is always about both offense and defense. The thing about fighting underwater is that you don't have as much mobility, and there are issues with defense. Sometimes the best way not to die is to not be somewhere."

"I'll keep that in mind if I ever get in a fight underwater," said Lily.

*She is like a little sponge, soaking in every bit of information around her.* Shay's phone came to life, and she pulled it out, expecting the Professor. Instead, it was Brownstone.

*What does he want?*

Shay searched her mind, trying to figure out if the bounty hunter had said he was going to call her. Maybe he'd pissed off some other international gang and needed to destroy their local headquarters.

She snickered. "What's up, Brownstone?" She held up her finger to her lips and looked at Lily.

"Alison has another Parents' Weekend, and I was wondering if you were going to go. It's this weekend, and she'd really like it if her Aunt Shay could be there."

Shay was still dealing with her feelings about being a part of this strange extended family, but she did like Alison. They'd bonded more during their recent time together.

If she hit Lake Michigan the following afternoon and recovered the stone, she could easily make it back in time for a weekend trip to Virginia.

Shay pondered the logistics for a moment. "What's your plan for the Parents' Weekend? You gonna take Alison on a barbeque tour of Virginia?"

Brownstone grunted. "Nope. She wants to experience a Broadway show, so I'm taking her to *Wicked* in New York."

"As in 'New York City?'"

"Yeah. There's only one Broadway, right?"

The tomb raider's stomach tightened. "Oh, that sounds cool, but I've got a job coming up, though, so you'll have to tell her I'm sorry. Maybe I can come during the next Parents' Weekend."

"Okay, no problem. Just thought I would ask."

"Thanks for asking, Brownstone. I appreciate it."

Shay ended the call and sighed.

Peyton stared at her.

"It's that school again, isn't it?" asked Lily, suspicious.

"This time, nothing about you. What?" Shay snapped. She didn't need Peyton seeing her in anything remotely resembling a vulnerable state.

"The Professor all but handed you the location of the stone." Peyton shrugged. "It'll probably take you longer to fly there and back than it will to recover it."

"Do you have a point, or are you just trying to annoy me?"

"That call was about Brownstone asking you to go somewhere this weekend, right?"

Shay shrugged. "He's taking Alison to New York. He wanted me to come along. So?"

"I don't get why you lied about being able to go," said Lily.

"Didn't you hear me? *New York!* It's too risky for me to go."

Peyton shook his head. "I thought you weren't worried? You told *me* not to worry."

Shay pointed to him and then her. "You were exposed on the East Coast for like five seconds in the middle of the night. I stole from an underworld courier and got in a gun battle in a subway, and, for that matter, more people are interested in seeing me dead in general. It's just too dangerous for me to go showing my face around NYC without a good reason."

"That's a lot of new information to take in," said Lily.

"Why didn't you tell him the truth, then?" asked Peyton.

"Brownstone doesn't need to know all my business. It's also why I've held back on telling him much about you or Lily." Shay shook her head. "Whatever. We don't have time to worry about taking a kid to a musical. I need to get ready to go to Lake Michigan."

Peyton shrugged. "Your choice. I'm going to go and see if I can find that missing amphibious jammer I mentioned yesterday."

"Good plan."

Shay sighed again once Peyton disappeared into the shelves with an annoying look on his face. Lily gave her a reassuring shrug like only a teenager can do and followed Peyton into the shelves.

In truth, she wanted to go to New York and spend time with both Brownstone and Alison. She wanted to tell him...

She wasn't even sure *what* she wanted to tell him. Maybe that she thought he did good work?

The tomb raider gagged at the thought. She didn't get what it was about the man that invaded her mind and refused to leave. She'd met plenty of tough and impressive people in her life, not to mention plenty of stubborn ones.

Introspection wasn't one of Shay's strong suits. Most of her life had been dedicated to professional killing. Hits were about action and reaction, not how she felt about the jobs. Feelings got in the way of being a good killer.

Tomb raids weren't all that psychological either. A well-executed tomb raid required research, bravery, and a reliable gun or two, not self-reflection. She'd managed to live her life without having to look into what motivated her— other than a desire to be the best, whether it was at killing or tomb raiding.

With Brownstone, though, she wanted to understand why she felt the way she did. She needed to understand. If she understood why she might manage to exert better control.

She'd done many things that didn't make sense to her. Things that gave her no advantage or reward. She'd never lived her life that way before.

Even when she'd saved Peyton she'd wanted an assistant out of it. She was willing to call him a friend now, but that didn't change her initial self-serving motivation.

In contrast, Shay had helped Brownstone attack the Harriken and kill Alison's father. She'd protected the girl and murdered two mercenaries who were targeting her.

Sure, she'd received money for the tomb raid in Mexico that had helped convince the Professor to give up the protective artifact, but it wasn't like Brownstone had paid her for any of the other things. She'd *chosen* to help— despite it being dangerous and stupid if she thought about it for too long.

*I'm supposed to be a pro. I'm supposed to help people when it's advantageous for me, not do people favors—especially those involving risking my life for someone like James Brownstone.*

Shay shook her head. She'd need to consider doing another mission with Brownstone. If this was all just some weird attraction, spending more time around him might cure her of it. Hell, it'd make the Professor happy for them to team up again as well.

Her stomach clenched at the alternative. Brownstone might be becoming something more than a partner to her.

*Shit. I don't know if that's good or bad.*

---

Shay stared at the stone oven as Peyton paced back and forth in front of it. "You do know that if this sucks, I'll be spending my entire time on the job thinking about terrible pizza. It might distract me at a critical moment. Bad pizza could get me killed."

"Give him a chance. He's been practicing on me and I'm still alive." Lily was wearing a Chanel sweater Shay recognized from the warehouse. She let it go. It was nice to see some of the clothes getting some use. Still, Peyton was rubbing off on the kid in some strange ways.

Peyton snorted. "Bad pizza might get you killed?"

"It's possible."

"Well, don't worry. I've had a lot more practice. I can guarantee this pizza won't get you killed."

"And how much of that practice involved sprinklers?" Shay inquired.

Peyton furrowed his brow. "Only the one time."

Lily held up two fingers.

Shay face-palmed. "You know, you might have to face the cold reality that you're just not meant to be a pizza man. We all have our strengths and weaknesses. It's not like I should be a life coach or a nun."

"Nope, I've got this. Every failure gives me new data, and I adjust. I'm closing in on the target." Peyton slid the paddle underneath the pizza and transferred it to the tray. "It's like anything else in life—just got to practice. I've been paying attention, traveling around, and having pizza all over LA. I've been looking at their ingredients and asking questions."

"Asking questions?" Shay raised an eyebrow. "And how did that go?"

"Surprisingly well, once I explained that I was an amateur trying to learn to cook at home. Most places I've asked have given me tips."

"Huh." Shay shrugged. "Okay, let's try it out, then. See if you actually applied any of those tips."

Peyton eagerly sliced the pepperoni pizza and placed a piece on a sandwich-sized paper plate. He handed it to Shay and awaited her verdict. Lily bit her lip, waiting for a sign.

Shay took several deep breaths and bit into the pizza. She tilted her head and chewed slowly. Good balance of flavors, good texture. No bizarre vinegar taste. She swallowed.

"I should pull my gun on you," she announced.

Peyton's shoulders slumped. "It's that bad?"

Shay laughed. "No, it's actually pretty good."

"Why pull your gun then?"

"Because you're obviously some wizard pretending to be Peyton."

The man smirked. "I'm no wizard. I'm the Pizza King." He high-fived Lily and strutted back and forth while Lily let out a whoop and held out her hands for a plate of pizza.

"Finally!" she exclaimed.

Shay snorted. "Not yet, you're not. More of a Pizza Squire, but if you have improved this much in such a short period, who the hell knows?"

"You're saying it was a good thing I bought the oven?"

"I didn't shoot you over it, did I?"

Peyton gave a piece to Lily and picked up a slice of the pizza and took a bite. His face lit up. "Damn, this is good!"

---

## 25

Shay parked her black rental van on the beach at the end of Montrose Avenue. The heavy cloud cover blocked the stars and the moon, but light from the high-rises on the other side of Michigan Avenue reflected off the water, slightly illuminating the beach.

If anyone wandered into the area they might not spot the van from a distance, but she still risked discovery.

Fortunately, at this time of night only the homeless and coyotes wandered the area, and the tomb raider hadn't spotted either of those. The icy cutting wind sweeping across Lake Michigan was more than enough to deter anyone without a strong reason to be there that night.

The tomb raider had chosen the location for that reason. It also provided a straight swim to the caves—*if* the Professor's information was correct, but she'd yet to go on a raid of his where that hadn't been the case.

The man might hold back information or twist words, but he'd never lied to her. At least not yet.

*Wonder what that first time will be about? Saving your ass, Smite-Williams, or saving mine?*

A little recon was in order. Caution always cut down on surprises, and cutting down on surprises tended to cut down on deaths.

Shay pulled a mini-drone from the back of the van and linked the visual feed to her AR goggles. She activated the machine and surveyed the area in the IR and visual bands. No people or surface animals, visible or otherwise, slept or walked anywhere near her location in either band.

"What, no invisible army? I'm almost disappointed."

She searched with the drone for a few more minutes. She not only sought high-temperature readings indicative of animals or people but also low temperatures that might be associated with ice magic. An additional five-minute sweep confirmed that Shay was alone.

"I didn't want to deal with that bitch yet anyway," she grumbled.

The tomb raider brought the drone down behind the truck and lifted her AR goggles. She proceeded to pull a cylindrical aquatic drone out of the back of the van.

The reflected light of the Chicago buildings might be enough to keep the area from being pitch-black, but that light would be worthless once she was a few feet under the water. Shay needed to make sure she knew exactly where she was going before she stepped one inch into the frigid water.

Besides, the way things had turned out for her on some recent raids, she wouldn't have been surprised if both the Loch Ness Monster or Ogopogo or angry mermaids popped out of the cave to try to eat her.

Such creatures had no reason to be in Lake Michigan, but neither did a strange alien stone. The world didn't make sense anymore, and the only way to keep her sanity was to accept that magic made cause and effect ambiguous.

Shay slipped the drone into the water and again lowered her AR goggles to watch the feed live. She waited until the machine was twenty feet down before activating its camera.

Its forward lights cut through the darkness as the drone continued to dive. The submersible approached the bottom and skimmed along for several minutes until a jagged opening appeared in the lake floor.

The tomb raider maneuvered the drone toward the rift for a better look. The crevice widened into a silt-lined cave angling down from the initial hole. The level of magic necessary to keep the massive amount of water above from pouring in stunned Shay.

She shook out her head and refocused on the job.

*Okay, I've confirmed the caves are there and there're no kraken around, but it's not like I can send an aquatic drone farther in. Guess it's time to go in myself.*

Shay brought the drone up and stored it in the back of the van before initiating the awkward process of putting on her cold-water diving equipment.

Sometimes she entertained the notion of training Peyton for field work and bringing him along if only to help her gear up in similar situations, like a squire helping his knight put on armor.

The problem was that easy raids with only mild environmental threats had grown increasingly rare compared to those that required gunplay or had extreme physical dangers. If Shay wanted the big money, she needed to take the big risks.

The tomb raider could. She'd trained for it most of her life, given her former profession. She didn't care how good Peyton might get at making pizza; he'd never have the levels of combat and physical skills necessary for her to feel comfortable with him watching her back.

Brownstone was one of the few men she'd ever encountered who did, even without his freaky magic amulet.

*Wonder if the bounty hunter would come along without a bounty as long as I cut him a percentage?*

Shay wasn't sure. Brownstone acted like he only cared about money at times, but his actions with Alison and his obsession with helping his church proved that the self-interest was more act than reality.

The tomb raider prepped her needle gun. She didn't anticipate a fight under the water, but she didn't want to get caught flatfooted if some water witch or angry rusalka decided they wanted to drown her ass.

The drone recon had shown that the caves would be large enough for her to enter even wearing all her diving equipment. She might be tough, but she couldn't free-dive hundreds of feet.

Shay geared up in her full-suit high-pressure wetsuit and diving equipment. It was expensive as hell, but it also let her surface much faster than more commercially available gear.

She waddled into the water with all the grace of an overweight penguin, taking step after step as the hungry waters of Lake Michigan rose higher on her body. Soon the water swallowed her whole.

Shay activated the lights on her mask and her wrist as she swam toward the cave entrance. Something darted past her and she spun, bringing up the needle gun. It wasn't a rusalka, Nessie, or a mercenary diver, just a large fish.

Seconds blurred into long minutes as she continued downward, now more attuned to the other inhabitants of the watery depths. She still occasionally swept the area with her lights to ensure only finned animals were in the area.

Shay arrived at the cave. The water rippled across the entrance, but none leaked inside.

She expected to feel some sort of jolt or strange warmth as she passed through the obvious magic of the entrance, but instead, her head passed into the cave without any sensation. Soon her entire body was inside.

The tomb raider stripped off her fins and bulkier gear. The Professor had provided coordinates to narrow down the location of the stone, but he hadn't been able to get it more specific than that. Time for a little exploration.

Shay double-checked to make sure she still had a few watertight pouches on her diving belt before hoisting the needle gun and moving farther into the cave.

*Why can't people hide their shit above the water?*

After fifteen feet or so Shay stopped. She'd had to access the cave via the water, which was held back by magic, but she wasn't having any trouble breathing. Another spell, perhaps, or some hidden access to the surface. It didn't matter in the end, but given all her adventures since becoming a tomb raider, it was hard to ignore all the subtle ways magic could influence her missions.

The coordinates pointed her to a cave that narrowed

into a separate tunnel, and Shay frowned. The low ceiling necessitated crawling, so she'd need to leave her weapon behind.

Shay shrugged. "Oh, well. Sometimes it's about having knife fights with alien demons, and sometimes it's about crawling through mud."

She dropped to her knees to crawl through the tight passage. A minute or two of careful travel brought her to an underground cavern that dwarfed the cave entrance, let alone the narrow tunnel leading to the cavern.

A small silver box sat near the back of the cavern.

"This is promising. Very promising."

Shay took slow, measured steps toward the box, still half-expecting an angry attack from some magical assassin or strange creature. The Professor had sworn up and down that the job would be simple, but he and his Light Elf buddy seemed awfully spooked by the situation.

If a man who'd been collecting artifacts for decades and a Light Elf were acting that way, there was no way in hell the artifact wasn't dangerous itself or being protected by someone or something dangerous.

The tomb raider patted her sheath. She'd not been able to bring her needle gun, but at least she still had one of the adamantine knives. She'd thought about bringing the others, but didn't want to risk the loss of all three under the cold waters of Lake Michigan should anything go wrong.

Shay's trip to the box preceded without any attacks, surprises, or anything of note. She let out a sigh of relief. Now, it was time for the next test.

She knelt in front of the box and took several deep breaths as her fingers hovered over the lid.

"One...two...three."

She raised the lid, and nothing exploded or shocked her. No giant boulders rolled out to crush her. She wasn't teleported to the World in Between. She didn't even have to deal with a poison dart.

The stone was inside the box and Shay stared at it, taking in all the fine details.

It was less worn than the one she'd recovered from Mexico, and as in the picture she'd been shown some of the glyphs were the same, but there were also several different ones.

Shay gently lifted the stone and settled it inside a pouch.

*So what are you and Correk hiding, Smite-Williams? Is this some secret Oriceran bullshit in the end?*

The tomb raider stood and shook her head. She wouldn't be able to just walk away from this job and be satisfied with her money. Whatever the Professor and the elf were doing might involve *her* stone.

Selling it to the Professor was one possibility but giving away her potentially historic proof for a little money struck her as pointless.

There also remained the question of whether the stone *itself* had some sort of magical power. She'd collected her knives and the *tachi,* but they weren't enough—not with the types of difficulties she had faced on many of her tomb raids.

If Shay didn't actively seek gear to protect herself from

dangerous magical foes, she'd be dead within the year. Yulia had proven that in Antarctica.

*I might not be a witch, but by the time I'm done they'll all be fucking afraid of me.*

She slammed the box closed, and a loud rumble shook the room.

"Oh…shit."

The cavern continued to shake. Jets of water shot from the wall and rocks fell from the ceiling.

Shay rushed toward the small tunnel. She dropped to her knees and hurried forward. Streams of water gushed from both sides of the tunnel, and sediment poured in from several new holes. When she'd crawled through the tunnel the first time, she'd only spotted a few puddles, now she splashed through several inches of frigid water.

Halfway through the tunnel, the silty water almost reached her chest. Three-quarters of the way through, her shoulders. Her pulse pounded in her ears as she crawled forward as fast as she could manage. The water and silt level kept rising.

Shay pushed forward, keeping her head up. The jagged rocky surface of the top of the tunnel sliced her forehead and blood ran down her face.

Mud and sediment dominated the water now, weighing down her limbs. She fought her way forward, keeping her head up as the water reached her chin.

A few seconds later the water swallowed her. She held her breath and closed her eyes as she struggled on. More sediment dumped into the tunnel, threatening to bury her alive.

*Fuck…this…noise.*

Shay emerged from the tunnel into the cave entrance. She rolled onto her back and gasped for air before sitting up.

Sand and mud had sealed the tunnel, an invisible wall holding in the water and silt.

"I really have to stop taking jobs that involve deep dives."

<hr />

Shay slid the briefcase containing the stone over to the Professor with a smile. "There was a trap, by the way. It wasn't so simple."

The elf wasn't with him this time, and neither was the tension. The rosy-cheeked man who was ready to turn into Father O'Banion after a few more beers had returned.

Smite-Williams took a long draw of his beer. "There's always something, now isn't there?"

"You still not gonna tell me what this is all about?"

"If you're half as clever as I think you are you won't need me to, Miz Carson." He winked.

"And Correk?"

"What about Correk?"

"Is he gonna come after me now?"

The Professor barked out a laugh. "And why would he do that?"

"Because I know too much? He had some sort of elven Man-in-Black vibe. I don't know." Shay shrugged.

"A lot of people in this world know too much these days." The Professor clucked his tongue. "The people responsible for holding back the truth of magic were never completely successful anyway. Don't worry about Correk. I'm sure if you see him again, he'll have come to help you. If you knew more about him, your opinion might change. He's a good man."

"There's much I don't know about a lot of the people who try to kill me. A lot of those might be considered good men."

The Professor scoffed. "Correk's not going to kill you."

"Maybe."

"Paranoia can be useful, Miz Carson, but only to a point."

She winked. "I'm not dead yet, so it's been pretty damned useful."

Shay locked eyes with the Professor, again considering telling him about her stone, but decided against it. If anything, he'd probably already reasoned out that she had a stone and was offering her plausible deniability from Correk and his Elf Mafia buddies or whoever he worked for.

If she admitted to having the stone, he'd probably have to call his Light Elf buddy, and he'd drag her off to whatever passed for an ultramax in Oriceran.

No, some secrets were worth keeping.

The tomb raider slowly stood and shook her head. "Thanks for the money. Except for the whole almost-being-buried-alive thing, it was a pretty easy job."

"Be well, Miz Carson, and know that every job you do for me does our world a service."

"Keep paying me and I don't care."

A smug smile played across the Professor's face. "Keep telling yourself that and maybe you'll eventually believe it."

An hour later Shay marched straight into the office in Warehouse Two. Osiris hissed at her and she glared at him.

"Don't tempt me, cat."

The cat hopped off Peyton's lap and strolled past Shay with all the arrogance of a reality show contestant.

Peyton looked up from his computer. "I've got good news."

"Tell me it doesn't involve you verifying that our sprinklers work again."

He shook his head. "Nope. I was running a comparative analysis on the symbols from your stone with the pictures you sent from the one you recovered from Lake Michigan and the one in the Project Nephilim data."

"And?"

"I think I might have a possible translation of the first two symbols. Even though the inscriptions are different on the three stones, the first two symbols are the same."

"Are you shitting me?"

Peyton shook his head. "I'm leaning heavily on some advanced language analysis and code-breaking neural nets that I, ahem, *borrowed* from the government, and a few other things. I don't understand the underlying algorithms, but I can still use the programs. I think the government guys couldn't make much progress because they only had the one sample, but we have three to work with and compare."

"And what is the translation?"

Peyton licked his lips. "Now, this is all very preliminary—"

"Just spit it the fuck out."

"Already here," he announced.

"Already here?"

"Yep. That's what they say. 'Already here.'"

Shay stared at the image of the three stones on the screen, her heart pounding. The words could mean a lot of things—and Peyton was relying on translation technology he didn't understand—but she didn't believe that changed either the potential message or the implications. There was only one question.

Who *was already here?*

Summer has arrived and it's time to take off those pounds I packed on all winter typing as fast as I could. At the time all that peanut butter and cheese and crackers seemed like a good idea. So quick and convenient. I'm rethinking that one.

Warm weather does that to me every year. I finally get motivated to get up and go outside, move around a little and I take stock of the shape I'm in. Lately, it's rounder... But not for long!

My life is changing – for the better and it's time I get it all in shape. I'm moving in about a month now into my dream house that's getting built. Writing as fast as I could about a swearing troll with Michael Anderle is what got me here.

But to really enjoy this next phase I have to pull it together and put down the chocolate.

Frankly, I want to do things differently this time and get all the corners of my life in fine working order. Physically, mentally, spiritually and financially. That's all of them, right?

I've been taking assessments of different things and become willing to look at areas I can improve with a lot of rigorous honesty. The biggest result is letting go of some entrenched habits, taking on some new ones and being willing to change and ask for help along the way.

I'll be honest – I'm 58 years old and entering the last large segment of my life.

If age brings wisdom, what I've figured out is that I can write it to be the way I want it to be. Only thing it's going to take is some hard-won courage mixed in with all that honesty and the willingness to just keep going. I'm looking forward to it... Kind of explains where the ideas for all those bad-ass women like Shay or Leira come from... right?

I'm off to keep writing my chapter – rewriting when necessary and making it just as bold as Shay's (without the killing parts and more easily letting people in to celebrate). I'll keep reporting back here in the author notes about the progress I make. Until then... enjoy the stories and thank you for being the best fans ever – very grateful! More adventures to follow.

I appreciate the fact that you worked your way through all of the book to make it here to my *Notes*!

Right now, I'm in La Puente, California. The birds are chirping and the temperature (according to SIRI) is 69 degrees with a light breeze. The sun hides behind some clouds and someone just exploded what sounds like a small stick of dynamite.

*WTF?*

The Author's Wife ™ explains that it is because Mexico beat Germany in the World Cup.

(Mexico – 1, Germany – 0)

In Texas, when you hear sounds that loud, someone was jacking around and fired a gun into the air. I'm in a neighborhood in a city. Normally, no one in Texas fires a gun into the air in the middle of a neighborhood inside a city.

Out in the country? *Sure, no problem.*

For the most part, this neighborhood is pretty quiet.

The birds are chirping, a baby is crying in the distance and I hear a dog barking.

Until a stick of dynamite is exploded... For a *soccer* game.

I know, I know, I should be 'meh' about this and I will get to that point. It was just a surreal experience - for the record I was talking with my Father here on Father's day out in the back yard, trying to coax him into coming to California to witness the packed earth, bricks, and stones that litter the backyard.

I think I was explaining that we had a 'blank canvas' with which to work. He could come over and provide me his thoughts on what I could do with it. You know, as I watch him go out and move a few things as he putters around fixing stuff, 'cause that is what my dad likes to do.

I don't think he bought it.

I'm going to have to futz with this backyard myself.

Well...*shit.*

I like to work out in the yard. *About two point three days in the year.* The rest of the time, I like to enjoy the yard. Working in the yard is *not* enjoyment.

Reading a book on a comfy chair out in the cool breeze is *enjoying* the yard. That I can do a hundred days out of the year.

Hmmph.

I'm apparently going to have to work harder, make more book money so that I can hire someone to futz around in my backyard.

Apparently, my Dad has seen that tactic somewhere before...

I wish ALL of you dads a Happy Father's Day (2018) and as long as this book is in print, and available have a massively great Father's Day for each of the years following!

Ad Aeternitatem,

Michael Anderle

### The Soul Stone Mage Series

#### * Sarah Noffke and Martha Carr *

House of Enchanted (1) - The Dark Forest (2) - Mountain of Truth (3) - Land of Terran (4) - New Egypt (5) - Lancothy (6) - Virgo (7)

### The Kacy Chronicles

#### * A.L. Knorr and Martha Carr *

Descendant (1) - Ascendant (2) - Combatant (3) - Transcendent (4)

### The Midwest Magic Chronicles

#### * Flint Maxwell and Martha Carr*

The Midwest Witch (1) - The Midwest Wanderer (2) - The Midwest Whisperer (3) - The Midwest War (4)

### The Fairhaven Chronicles

#### * with S.M. Boyce *

Glow (1) - Shimmer (2) - Ember (3) - Nightfall (4)

# CONNECT WITH THE AUTHORS

**Martha Carr Social**

Website: http://www.marthacarr.com

Facebook: https://www.facebook.com/
groups/MarthaCarrFans/

**Michael Anderle Social**

Website: http://kurtherianbooks.com/

Email List: http://kurtherianbooks.com/email-list/

Facebook Here: https://www.
facebook.com/TheKurtherianGambitBooks/